Mahabl

The Eternal Epic in Short Stories

Vignes Chandran

INDIA · SINGAPORE · MALAYSIA

Notion Press

No. 8, 3rd Cross Street,
CIT Colony, Mylapore,
Chennai, Tamil Nadu - 600 004

First Published by Notion Press 2020
Copyright © Vignes Chandran 2020
All Rights Reserved.

ISBN 978-1-64919-530-2

This book has been published with all efforts taken to make the material error-free after the consent of the author. However, the author and the publisher do not assume and hereby disclaim any liability to any party for any loss, damage, or disruption caused by errors or omissions, whether such errors or omissions result from negligence, accident, or any other cause.

While every effort has been made to avoid any mistake or omission, this publication is being sold on the condition and understanding that neither the author nor the publishers or printers would be liable in any manner to any person by reason of any mistake or omission in this publication or for any action taken or omitted to be taken or advice rendered or accepted on the basis of this work. For any defect in printing or binding the publishers will be liable only to replace the defective copy by another copy of this work then available.

FOR K. SAMBHAVIY;

ENJOY THE BOOK!

— VIG —

To Krishna,

to many the very reason of existence,
to me my confidante, guide and inspiration.
I live only with the dream of reuniting with you,
when You decide that the time is right.

Lust, anger, and greed-these constitute the threefold gate of hell, leading to the destruction of the soul's welfare. These three, therefore, man should abandon.

Bhagavad Gita 16:21

The truly wise mourn neither for those who are living, nor for those who have passed away.

Bhagavad Gita 2:11

All know the way; few actually walk it.

Bodhidharma

God is in all men, but all men are not in God; that is why we suffer.

Swami Ramakrishna

Wanting to reform the world without discovering one's true self is like trying to cover the world with leather to avoid the pain of walking on stones and thorns. It is much simpler to wear shoes.

Ramana Maharishi

Contents

Foreword 9
Prologue 11

Part One: The Beginning

How It All Began 15

The Story of Amba and Bhishma 21

Birth of the Pandavas 27

The Emergence of Dronacharya 33

How Arjuna Became Drona's Favourite 39

A Game of Dice 45

The Insult of Draupadi 51

Part Two: In Exile and Beyond

The Pandavas Exiled 59

Arjuna Obtains Celestial Weapons 65

Contents

Bhima Meets Hanuman 73

How Krishna Became Arjuna's Charioteer................81

Krishna Advocates Peace............................ 87

A Mother's Dilemma 93

Karna Promises....................................... 99

Part Three: The War

The Great War Begins................................ 109

Bhishma Vanquished.................................117

Valiant Abhimanyu 123

A Test of Character.................................. 129

The Death of Karna 135

The Great War Ends 141

Krishna Chooses to Leave 151

For the Love of a Dog 159

Every Beginning Has an End 165

Epilogue..169
Glossary..173
Acknowledgements....................................193

FOREWORD

All glories to Krishna, from whom everything began and will end, and causes all of existence to revolve as they do.

It has always been a dream of mine ever since I picked up this epic called the Mahabharata during my teenage years to be able to write my own version, and here I am today, presenting you with the results of my efforts. It is my greatest wish that you thoroughly enjoy the stories within this great epic that showcased not only traits such as loyalty, love and friendships but also deception, revenge and envy.

The Mahabharata and the Ramayana are the two great Indian epics familiar to us in this age, and although the latter was one that happened earlier, it remains hugely popular within today's population. This is, in my opinion, due to the far simpler story line and relatively fewer number of characters within the Ramayana when you compare it with the Mahabharata.

The Mahabharata on the other hand is slowly being overlooked and forgotten, with many generally struggling with the sheer size of the story and the numerous characters associated with the epic.

Understanding this struggle, I have made it my mission to make this story well-known once again not only for this generation but also for the generations to come, by producing a compact, condensed version that anyone could read. It is too great an epic to be allowed to vanish, and I hope this book (and hopefully subsequent books) will assist to keep the story alive.

It is believed that the original Mahabharata was written by Lord Ganesha himself under the dictation of Sage Vyasa, and I thank Krishna for the guidance and ability to write a portion of what my namesake has written all those years ago. I remain merely the tool.

I have chosen a number of stories from the epic, mainly my own favourites, to re-tell in my own words. I have also provided simplified narratives of the rest of the epic in between these short stories to ensure that every reader understands the Mahabharata in entirety by reading this book.

You might find that there are discrepancies between this version compared to the previous versions of the epic that you might have read; these differences are deliberate and completely-based on my own opinion on how the great story turned out.

I have attempted to make my version of the Mahabharata to be as simple and compact as I am able to. I sincerely hope that you will enjoy this book as much as I have enjoyed writing it, which was immensely.

Be prepared now to be transported into an ancient world of mystic, emotions and ultimately battle, where some of the greatest lessons of life can be found.

Prologue

Duryodhana looked across the battlefield. This was not how it was supposed to end.

He was supposed to be invincible in battle. He had three invincible warriors leading the army on his side. The likes of Bhishma, Drona and Karna did not know the meaning of defeat in battle, and he had the strength of all three, combined. But all three had been vanquished, against all odds, and have reached the heavenly regions of slain warriors.

He had eleven full divisions at his disposal, but what remained now was just a handful of soldiers who looked at loss at best, without a competent general to lead the line.

Duryodhana's head grew heavier, struggling to accept the reality before him. On the brink of defeat, how difficult to digest were those words.

He saw a glimmer of light from the camp of the Pandavas, and his eyes strained to make sense of what he was looking at. The light grew brighter and brighter, and slowly but surely Duryodhana could make out the shape of a face, seemingly being lit up magically by a divine ray. A face that was looking directly back at him, smiling his signature boyish smile, the very same smile that had captivated countless. Duryodhana witnessed Krishna nod slightly at him, with the smile bearing traces of sadness, as if telling Duryodhana that it is almost time to say goodbye. For the final time.

And then it dawned upon him.

It had always been, and always will be Krishna. The sole reason of why he, the son of Dhritarastra, is on the brink of losing the battle of his life.

The only reason of why he was now standing on his own, devoid of his unconquerable generals, facing a lonely fight for a kingdom he no longer had any desire for.

If only he had chosen Krishna when he was given the chance to.

If only.

Part One

The Beginning

HOW IT ALL BEGAN

Slightly more than 5000 years ago, lived great King Shantanu. Shantanu was the undisputed monarch of the Kuru dynasty, and although it was not known at that time, he would eventually prove to be the ancestor of the history-altering Pandavas and Kauravas. Considered a very-worthy descendent of the famed Bharata race, Shantanu governed his kingdom in a just, peaceful manner, keeping all enemies at bay and the kingdom prosperous. He will one day fall in love with a maiden that he met by the holy Ganges, who will agree to marry him and bear him children, on the condition that he never questions any of her actions, failing of which she will leave him and never be seen again.

Gladly agreeing at first, Shantanu will be filled with both helpless guilt and utter horror as his wife would drown their newly-born babies, one after another. When the eighth new-born was about to be drowned in the same manner, the king could bear it no longer and stopped his wife, despite his promise not to.

He would then discover the true nature of his wife, who was actually goddess Ganga that accepted human form to help a group of celestial beings to be rid of a curse, obtained for stealing from sage Vasistha. Ganga then made her way back to the river where she came from, taking the baby with her but promising to return after a few years.

The painful loss of his wife was simply unbearable, until one day when Ganga reappeared with a radiant-looking child, their son Devavrata. Trained in martial arts by incomparable Parasurama himself and in Vedic scriptures by Vasistha, Devavrata shone without compare in prowess and character, displaying skills and knowledge unheard of for someone his age.

Bidding goodbye to the king, Ganga then passed on the responsibility of bringing up their son to Shantanu and left, never to be seen again. Shantanu returned to his capital, Hastinapura where he would spend his days governing his kingdom with his son who would in time be named heir to the throne.

Shantanu did not entertain the thought of re-marrying again in memory of Ganga, until one fateful day when he comes across beautiful Satyavati while walking by the Yamuna. Losing his heart to the beauty and grace of the damsel, Shantanu was eager for her to be his queen, and met her father, the chief fishermen of a nearby village.

Seeing the king's strong desire to wed his daughter, Satyavati's father agreed to the union, albeit with one condition; that the child borne by his daughter would be the successor to the Hastinapura throne. As much as he desired Satyavati, Shantanu could not bring himself to deny the godly Devavrata from his birth right and rightful future as the king, and left empty-handed back to his palace.

Devavrata would learn of this incident from father's charioteer, and seeking to make his father happy, would approach Satyavati and her father. He would give his word to the both of them that the son of Shantanu and Satyavati would be monarch instead of him, to which Satyavati's father replied, "Noble prince, while I fully trust your word and know that you will not lay claim to the throne, what assurance do I have that your children will not once you have passed on? Being more god than human, very few would be able to resist you in battle, and your children will undoubtedly be in the same mould. This poses a great risk to the future children of Satyavati, in case your descendants decide to rebel and lay claim to the throne. I cannot allow this marriage to happen while this danger exists."

To which Devavrata responded without hesitation, "Dear sir, your worries are without doubt valid. Not only will I renounce my claim to the throne, I will from this moment undertake an oath of celibacy that will remain in action as long as I am alive. I also pledge to be of service to the throne of Hastinapura to the best of my abilities for as long as this body is able, this I promise! Nothing is more important to me than the happiness of my father, and I would do anything it takes to see a smile on his face again." From that moment onwards, the name Devavrata was simply forgotten, replaced by one that is much more striking; Bhishma, which means one that undertakes a terrible vow and fulfils it.

When love-struck Shantanu heard of what had happened, his joy knew no bounds. He blessed his first son with the Icchamrityu boon, one that allowed Bhishma to select his own time of death, automatically making Bhishma invincible unless he chose to leave his mortal body himself.

The marriage of Shantanu and Satyavati was finalized in due time, and duly celebrated by everyone in the kingdom that were eager to see the king happy again with a queen by his side.

From the joyful nuptial of Shantanu and Satyavati, two princes were born, namely Chitrangada and Vichitravirya. Satyavati would, prior to her marriage to Shantanu, have an offspring as well in the form of the sage Vyasa through a union with the storyteller Parasara. However, she would regain her womanhood after conceiving this divine child on the banks of the Yamuna river. Vyasa will grow into one of the greatest sages the world has seen as well as the renowned compiler of the Mahabharata, famously-captured by Lord Ganesha under the dictation of the sage.

    Both Chitrangada and Vichitravirya would grow up to be strong-willed, handsome young men, loved by all. The elder son Chitrangada would succeed his father to the throne at Hastinapura, ruling for quite some time before he unexpectedly angers a gandharva king of the same name (Chitrangada). The misunderstanding would boil up into a full-fledged battle that lasted a full three years, before Hastinapura's king is disastrously-killed without a son to his name. Thus, in tragic circumstances, younger brother Vichitravirya takes control of the beautiful kingdom of Hastinapura.

The Story of Amba and Bhishma

The younger prince, Vichitravirya would prove to be a worthy king in the later days of his kingship, however he remained a child when his elder brother was slain in battle. Thus, Bhishma ruled the kingdom as the regent until Vichitravirya attained governing age. During this period is when the king of Kasi decided to hold a swayamwara for his three daughters; Amba, Ambika and Ambalika.

All three princesses were well-known for their beauty and gracefulness, thus princes from neighbouring kingdoms flocked to Kasi to take part in the event, eager to win the hands of the princesses. Realizing that Vichitravirya was of marriageable age, Bhishma decided to make his way to Kasi to win the hands of the princesses on behalf of Vichitravirya. Bhishma feared for the safety of the young king if there were battles to be fought, as these swayamwara occasions usually turn out to be fairly-fiery affairs. When the other princes realized the invincible Bhishma had come to the swayamwara to compete, they were dejected as they knew that he was a peerless warrior, and they stood no chance against him. Not knowing that he had come to win the princesses for

Vichitravirya, some of the princes talked faultily of him and reminded him of his oath of celibacy, stinging Bhishma into a furious state. This resulted in him challenging the whole assembly of princes to a test of manhood, defeating each and every one of them and carrying all three princesses away without any resistance.

Amba's lover, Salva will be part of the contingent of princes that came to win the hands of the princesses, and he was humiliated and defeated just like the others, not able to withstand the prowess of mighty Bhishma. While in the chariot on the way back to Hastinapura, Amba would request for Bhishma to release her as she had already given her heart to Salva, and could not think of marrying anyone other than him.

Bhishma relented and allowed Amba to return to Kasi. However, the shamed Salva refused to accept Amba as his wife, saying, "As much as I love you, how can I accept you as my wife before the very citizens that watched me disgraced in a battle to win you? Standing here dejected and shamed, I cannot accept you as my wife." Amba was distraught with the turn of events, and seeing no other way, made her way to Hastinapura where preparations were in full swing to celebrate the marriage of the young king with Ambika and Ambalika. Here she asked Vichitravirya to accept her as his wife as well, however fate had other plans webbed. The young prince refuses Amba, as he could not bear marrying someone who has her heart set on another. Thus rejected twice, and in desperation, Amba returns to Salva and begs for him to marry her, which he refuses to.

Disconsolate Amba, seeing no other option, turns to Bhishma and blames him for her predicament, "O Son of

Ganga, it is by your actions alone that I am in this predicament today. Redeem yourself and marry me, and release me from this sorrow that I am currently enduring." Bhishma, despite feeling extremely sorry for Amba, could not give up his oath and refuses Amba. Thus rejected by three different men, Amba burned with anger, full of wrath towards Bhishma for causing her unspeakable anguish. Forsaking all thoughts of marriage and fuelled only by thoughts of revenge, she looked for a warrior that could defeat Bhishma in battle. Long and hard was her journey, and when all human options failed her, she performed penances and pleased Lord Muruga, who appeared before her and provided her with a garland of flowers, saying that the wearer of the garland would have the ability to slay Bhishma in battle.

With renewed hope, she sought in vain many warriors who all refused her advances in fear of Bhishma. Frustrated, she found King Drupada who also refused to champion her cause. She left the garland of flowers on the gates of his palace and retired to the forest where she found sages advising her to look for Parasurama. Following their advice, Amba found Parasurama who was extremely moved by her story and agreed to challenge Bhishma to an assessment of battle skills.

Parasurama is actually Vishnu-reincarnate, armed with the holy mission of clearing the lands of unworthy kshatriyas. Parasurama also served as the teacher of Bhishma in weaponry when the latter was in his youth. The battle between master and student hence commenced, and it raged long and hard, both men marvelling at the competency and abilities of the other. One arrow was thwarted by another, while an astra was extinguished by one more deadly.

Firstly they fought with the bow, then the sword, next the mace, and finally they wrestled with bare hands. The fight was such a wonderful spectacle that it was said that the gods themselves came to watch, lasting for well over twenty days as Parasurama was an immortal while Bhishma had been granted a boon by his father that allowed him to choose his own time of death, an act that also gives immortality on its own accord.

After weeks of battling each other, finally Bhishma invoked a mysterious celestial weapon that was unknown to Parasurama, obtained from his ancestors. However, before launching the weapon on Parasurama, a divine voice would intervene and warn Bhishma against using the weapon against his guru as it would cause Parasurama severe humiliation. Bhishma would heed the words of the divine voice, and stopped short of mounting the weapon upon his bow.

Bearing witness to this, Parasurama acknowledged defeat, and full of pride for his disciple, would bless Bhishma profusely before announcing him as the winner of the battle. Having failed Amba, Parasurama consoled her by saying that although no living human would be able to kill Bhishma, he would bless her with a boon that would allow her to receive the grace of Lord Shiva, who would aid her in getting the revenge that she craved for. Through terrible penances and the power of the boon bestowed by Parasurama, Amba's austerities would be rewarded by a pleased Shiva, who blessed her with the ability to slay Bhishma in her next life. Unable to wait any longer, Amba launched herself into the fire, and will be reborn as the daughter of king Drupada. The garland of flowers would still be hanging at the gates of the palace, and the reborn Amba would place it around her neck, much to the distress of her father who banished her from the kingdom as he was very much afraid of Bhishma's wrath.

The same Amba would then transform into a male warrior named Sikhandin after spending years training in the forest, and would eventually cause the death of Bhishma during the terrible war of Kurukshetra many, many years later, as Bhishma would refuse to attack the female-born Sikhandin even when his life was at stake.

Allow us to return to Hastinapura now and see how the royal family was progressing.

A few years after the marriage of Vichitravirya to Ambika and Ambalika, tragedy would strike the young king who would succumb to an illness, leaving the revered monarchy without a king. As Bhishma was sworn to celibacy, while both Chitrangada and Vichitravirya died without progeny, Satyavati and Bhishma called her first-born Vyasa back from the mountains to help continue the royal lineage through unions with the queens; first with Ambika and then Ambalika. Ambika recoiled in disgust when she saw Vyasa in his unkempt state, and kept her eyes closed during union; not being able to bear the sight of him, thus the son they produced, Dhritarastra, was born blind.

Ambalika on the other hand turned pale when she saw Vyasa, and this resulted in their son, Pandu, being born pale. In time brave Pandu, who excelled in both weaponry and Vedic knowledge, became king of the monarchy. Dhritarastra was side-lined due to blindness, leaving him furious. Once they were of marriageable age, Pandu married Kunti and Madri while Dhritarastra married Gandhari. Wanting to share the exact same pleasures and struggles as her husband, Gandhari would blindfold herself for life after her marriage with Dhritarastra.

Due to a rishi's curse Pandu would not be able to obtain children in the normal manner, while Dhritarastra and Gandhari were blessed with 101 children; 100 sons and 1 daughter, the eldest of which being Duryodhana.

Let us now see how the illustrious Pandavas were born despite of their father's curse.

Birth of the Pandavas

Due to a rishi's curse during an ill-fated hunting excursion, Pandu would not be able to obtain children in the usual manner, plunging the kingdom into distress. Unsure of how to ensure the continuity of his illustrious lineage and wanting to redeem himself for the sin that he had committed, Pandu would proceed to exile himself to the forest, leaving the administration of the kingdom to Bhishma and Vidura.

Kunti and Madri steeled themselves and willingly accepted the same fate as their husband, despite Pandu's attempts to discourage them from joining him in the forest. And while the peaceful nature of the jungle did give him the serenity that his heart required, the worry of being childless continued to torture his soul.

Unable to see her husband, the famed monarch of the Kuru dynasty, tormented in such agony every day and constantly pining for children, Kunti disclosed the secret of a boon that she received from sage Durvasa during her younger days. The boon would allow her to invoke any deity of choice to beget a child from them, leaving her pure again after the spiritual union. Pandu was ecstatic when he heard of Kunti's boon, not only in the knowledge that his lineage could now be continued, but also realizing that sons born of gods would be far greater than those fathered by mortals such as himself.

Blessing his lucky stars, Pandu then asked Kunti to firstly invoke the god of righteousness and justice, Dharma. Also known to the mortals as Yama, Pandu knew that a son fathered by the lord of justice would be as sinless and steadfast to dharma as his godly father, making him the perfect choice as the next-in-line as king of the Kuru dynasty.

Agreeing to Pandu's wish, Kunti invoked Lord Dharma who appeared almost immediately. Understanding the queen's wish for a child, Dharma united with her in spirit before restoring her womanhood. In due time, Kunti will conceive and give birth to a bright baby boy resplendent like Dharma himself.

A voice was heard from the skies blessing the moderately-sized baby at the time of birth, "Behold the birth of Yudhisthira, born of divine union and blessed to be of blameless character and utmost righteousness. This boy will one day rule the world, and will not divert from the path of dharma regardless of the temptation." Both Pandu and Kunti were elated to hear the blessing from the skies, and the king lost his anxiousness of not having a son in no time.

As Yudhisthira approached his first birthday, Pandu and Kunti agreed that it would be beneficial for the kingdom to also have a prince of supernatural strength to complement the knowledge and righteousness as their first born. Choosing the incomparable god of wind, Vaayu as the deity of choice this time, Kunti invoked the strongest god with the same mantra given by Durvasa.

Unable to resist the call of the mantra, Vaayu appeared before Kunti and knowing her intention, instantly blessed her with a son comparable to himself. In time Kunti will conceive and produce a booming baby who proved to be a giant even during birth. The same voice will be heard like thunder from the skies, announcing, "Behold Bhima, the strongest and most powerful amongst men." Bhima gave his parents immense joy through his loud, playful character, though he did have a huge appetite, larger than even those of adults!

Another couple of years passed by, and Pandu asked Kunti to approach Lord Indra, the god of the demigods himself to bless them with another prince. Pandu wanted another son that was not only physically-able but also devoted to the Supreme, just like how Indra was devoted to Vishnu. Before invoking Indra, both Pandu and Kunti took a vow of asceticism in order to please the god of the heavens. After almost a year, Indra was pleased by the conduct of both Pandu and Kunti, and understanding their request asked Kunti to invoke him with the child-bearing boon.

In time great Arjuna was born to the proud parents, and the same heavenly voice was heard decreeing for a third time, "Behold Arjuna, one that will not only equal the great god Shiva in dexterity and valour, but will also help to turn your kingdom into one as splendid as Indra's Amaravathi. This baby will also be the most ardent of devotees of Lord Vishnu, and will please the Supreme Lord immensely throughout his life, forever living in his blessings."

Besides themselves with joy, the parents splashed love and care on baby Arjuna who was magnificent in appearance like Indra himself. It was also noted that Arjuna was greatly devoted to his parents and elder brothers even since a baby. Arjuna will eventually become Lord Krishna's greatest devotee, their relationship often compared to the divine Nara and Narayana themselves.

While Kunti now had three sons to call her own, Pandu realized that his other queen Madri had none, causing her much distress. Wanting to be fair to both of his queens, the compassionate Pandu requested for Kunti to share the secret mantra with Madri to allow her to have a child of her own as well. The ever-gracious Kunti was happy to oblige, even more so as she did not want to bear any more children. Reciting the mantra on behalf of Madri, Kunti asked the younger queen to think of her deity of choice.

Madri, being slightly insecure and uncertain of having the same opportunity of utilizing the mantra again, opted for the twin Ashwini stars as her deity of choice, resulting in her conceiving and giving birth to two princes of gorgeous complexion. During the birth of the princes, the heavenly voice was heard announcing, "Behold Nakula and Sahadeva, equal to their fathers, the Ashwini twins, in beauty and attractiveness, and in time will become heroes full of valour, energy and knowledge."

Pandu now lived in contentment, happy with the knowledge that both of his queens have children of their own, and that he now had five illustrious sons of godly-nature to continue his legacy. The five sons of Pandu would eventually be world-renowned as the Pandavas.

Life in the forest with his wives and young sons was satisfying for Pandu, until one day when he succumbed to the combined temptation of spring, Madri and the rishi's curse, falling down dead the moment he felt the pleasure of the bed. Believing to be the cause of Pandu's untimely death, Madri would then jump into the same fire that cremated Pandu's body, leaving Kunti with the sole responsibility of bringing up five young princes.

Finding an anguish-stricken Kunti with five young boys seemingly unsure of what to do next, the hermits of the forest brought them back to Hastinapura, where the queen and her children were reunited with Vidura and Bhishma. Bhishma immediately took the orphaned princes under his wings, while Gandhari and Dhritarastra attempted to pacify Kunti. The whole kingdom mourned the passing of the much-loved Pandu and his queen Madri.

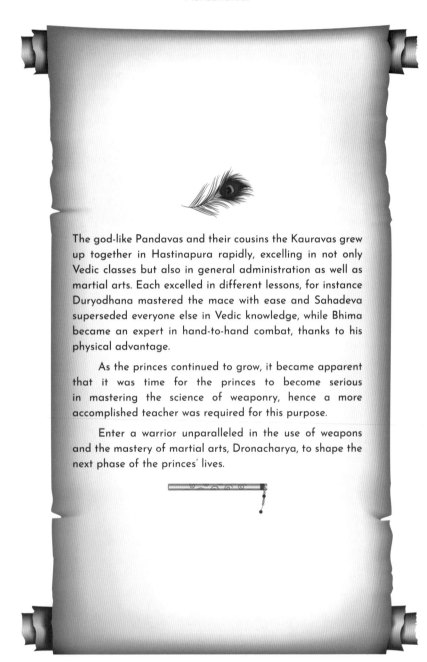

The god-like Pandavas and their cousins the Kauravas grew up together in Hastinapura rapidly, excelling in not only Vedic classes but also in general administration as well as martial arts. Each excelled in different lessons, for instance Duryodhana mastered the mace with ease and Sahadeva superseded everyone else in Vedic knowledge, while Bhima became an expert in hand-to-hand combat, thanks to his physical advantage.

As the princes continued to grow, it became apparent that it was time for the princes to become serious in mastering the science of weaponry, hence a more accomplished teacher was required for this purpose.

Enter a warrior unparalleled in the use of weapons and the mastery of martial arts, Dronacharya, to shape the next phase of the princes' lives.

The Emergence of Dronacharya

The eternal warrior Drona is well-recognized as an unrivalled weapon-master and teacher of martial arms. The son of sage Bharadwaj, the commanding warrior completed his studies of the Vedas even in his adolescence. And despite being a brahmana himself, he subsequently devoted his life to the skill of archery, becoming an unmatched archer even in his youth.

Drona received instructions on weaponry and archery from renowned gurus such as Agnivesha and Parasurama. Armed with such knowledge, Drona became an unrivalled wielder of weapons and struck fear in the hearts of all his enemies until the day of his death. Despite that, he remained humble and did not seek for riches or money as he had no use for them. It was at the hermitage where he taught archery that he became close to Drupada, the young crown-prince of the Panchala kingdom whose king was the friend of Drona's father, Bharadwaj. Both youthful companions were taken by each other and went on to become extremely close friends, and Drupada, in his youthful playfulness, would promise to give half of his kingdom to Drona once he became king.

Drona eventually married the sister of Kripa, and they were blessed with a son whom they called Ashwatthama. Drona was extremely fond of his son and wife, and now with a family to look after and provide for, was forced to seek for material support for his family. He first went to Parasurama who was distributing his riches before retiring to the forest, however Drona arrived a little too late and Parasurama had already completely given away all his riches.

Desiring to do something for Drona, Parasurama will impart all of his knowledge of weapons to Drona before leaving. Already a master of weaponry, the knowledge imparted by Parasurama left Drona virtually invincible in battle as he now possessed the added knowledge of celestial weapons as well. Nevertheless he was still in need of wealth, thus he continued his journey. Remembering his old friend Drupada who was now the king of Panchala, Drona visited his kingdom hoping to be treated generously as promised by Drupada during their youth. However, his hopes were shattered by a very different Drupada, arrogant with wealth and power, who scorned Drona when the weapon-master introduced himself to the king.

Sneering, Drupada said, "O sage, how can you, a wandering beggar be a friend to a king such as myself? Friendship you call it? With all your knowledge, do you not realize that friendship may only exist between two equals? How can you, a wandering beggar, be a friend to me, the ruler of a kingdom?" Insulted thus, Drona left Drupada's kingdom with anger burning his heart, vowing for revenge. The lesson here states that even the best of men suffers from weaknesses such as anger and arrogance, such is the nature of humans.

The Emergence of Dronacharya

Having been insulted by an old friend drunk in arrogance, Drona continued on his quest for riches, eventually finding it through employment at Hastinapura where the young Pandavas and Kauravas were growing up. Here his brother-in-law Kripacharya served as the preceptor of the kingdom, and one day while the young Pandavas were playing in the park, a ball as well as Yudhisthira's ring accidentally fell into the well.

Unable to retrieve both items, the boys looked around for help and came across Drona who was watching them, smiling at their predicament. Embarrassed at their failure to accomplish such a simple task despite being princes from a distinguished line of kings, the princes, led by Yudhisthira asked Drona to help them retrieve the ball, promising him a meal at the palace in return. Still smiling, Drona took a blade of grass and recited some invocation mantras that transformed the blade of grass into an arrow which flew into the well, striking the ball which in return rebounded to the top of the well. Spellbound by the wonder they just witnessed; the boys begged Drona to retrieve the ring as well.

Drona borrowed a bow and an arrow, shot the arrow clean through the well opening, striking the ring right at the bottom of the well and causing it to rebound straight into the hand of the grateful Yudhisthira. Full of admiration of the mysterious brahmana, the princes rushed back to the palace to relay the news of his appearance to grandfather Bhishma. When the grandsire heard of the tale of the brahmana, he knew for certain that they could only be talking about valorous Drona. Recognizing the opportunity, Bhishma decided that Dronacharya was the most suitable person to impart further knowledge to the princes in terms of military education and training. Receiving Drona with all respect, Bhishma then appoints him as the chief instructor at Hastinapura with the responsibility of educating the princes in weaponry. Thus did Drona find employment, and succeeds in acquiring wealth for the benefit of his wife and son. After several months of training, Drona will instruct both the Kauravas (led by Duryodhana) and the Pandavas (led by Arjuna) to capture the arrogant Drupada and bring him back to Drona, alive. Duryodhana would fail miserably and returned disgraced to Hastinapura after being routed by Drupada and his forces. Next went Arjuna who displayed great skill and dexterity to achieve the target of seizing Drupada and bringing him back to Drona successfully. Drona would be extremely pleased by Arjuna's triumph, and would bless him profusely for this achievement.

Drona then addressed Drupada, "Dear Drupada, I have captured you here today not to kill you, but to remind you of the importance of humility and friendship. When we were younger, I remember us being the best of friends but after you became king, you chose to forget the past and dishonour me when I came seeking your friendship. You insulted me by calling me a beggar and reminded me that friendship can only materialize between equals. See my friend, I am now equally a king like you, having conquered your kingdom. Will you accept my friendship now? I shall return half your kingdom to you, and may we be friends like before once again."

Drona then returned half the kingdom to Drupada, at the same time freeing him and treating him with the respect a king deserves. Humbled and defeated, Drupada returned to what is left of his kingdom in shame, vowing retaliation in return for the humiliation that he had suffered. In a frenzy of hatred, craving for revenge, Drupada lived a life of austerities and tapas and underwent numerous difficulties to receive the grace of the gods to be granted a son and a daughter that would successfully end the life of his sworn enemy; Drona.

His efforts would not go in vain, as the gods would be pleased with his austerities and will bless him with a son, Dhrishtadyumna who would eventually command the Pandava forces at the battle of Kurukshetra, as well as a daughter, Draupadi, who would wed not only Arjuna but all the Pandavas. It is well-known that the people most dear to Dronacharya was firstly his son, Ashwatthama and secondly, Arjuna. It was said that Drona's affection towards Arjuna was such that sometimes he displayed more love and attention towards Arjuna compared to even Ashwatthama. However, Drona's nurturing of Arjuna to such extents proved to be his own downfall as Arjuna would go on to become one of the very few select warriors that could face Drona in battle, culminating in the death of Drona himself a few days after he takes the command of the Kaurava forces at Kurukshetra.

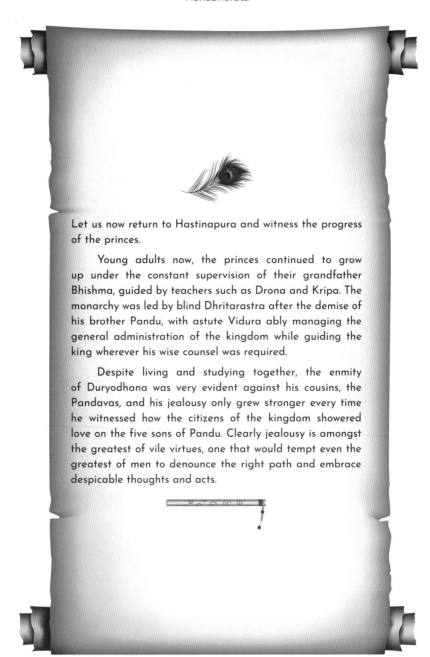

Let us now return to Hastinapura and witness the progress of the princes.

Young adults now, the princes continued to grow up under the constant supervision of their grandfather Bhishma, guided by teachers such as Drona and Kripa. The monarchy was led by blind Dhritarastra after the demise of his brother Pandu, with astute Vidura ably managing the general administration of the kingdom while guiding the king wherever his wise counsel was required.

Despite living and studying together, the enmity of Duryodhana was very evident against his cousins, the Pandavas, and his jealousy only grew stronger every time he witnessed how the citizens of the kingdom showered love on the five sons of Pandu. Clearly jealousy is amongst the greatest of vile virtues, one that would tempt even the greatest of men to denounce the right path and embrace despicable thoughts and acts.

How Arjuna Became Drona's Favourite

As the years went by the Pandavas and Kauravas received their education from various teachers, none more than from Dronacharya. Drona became the preceptor of the Kurus as well as many other princes from other kingdoms who heard news of his school of martial arts in Hastinapura and flocked there in the thousands to receive his wisdom.

Drona nurtured and watched his students excel in different skills, for instance Nakula became a great swordsman while none superseded Arjuna's skills with the bow and arrow. Now stably-employed, Drona lived in Hastinapura with his wife and son Ashwatthama in comfort; with the Kuru Dynasty more than happy to fulfil his needs in exchange for the incomparable knowledge that he imparts.

The princes were constantly tested by Drona via competitions that test not only skill, strength and knowledge but as importantly also their levels of focus. In one such instance, Drona chose to test his students using the bird eye trial. With Yudhisthira, Duryodhana, Arjuna, Bhima and the rest of the princes in attendance, Drona attached a hanging wooden bird on a branch of a nearby tree, and brought the princes a fair distance away from the target before asking the question, "Students, I want you to strike the eye of the bird with your arrow. Tell me now, what do you see?"

Yudhisthira, being the eldest Pandava, replied, "Master, I see the bird, the tree and the blue sky." Drona was unhappy with his answer and stopped the arrow, citing, "You will not hit the target, you lack the required focus." Next in line was Duryodhana, whose reply was, "Acharya, I see you standing in front of me and behind you I see the tree, the bird and my target, the bird's eye." Drona could not hide his displeasure over the answer and forbade Duryodhana from shooting as well.

The likes of Bhima, Vikarna, Sahadeva and Nakula also provided unsatisfactory answers until it was Arjuna's turn to shoot the arrow. Drona enquired, "Tell me Arjuna, what do you see?"

Arjuna's answer was crisp, "Master, I see the eye of the bird and nothing else. May I shoot my arrow?". With a smile, Drona accepted Arjuna's answer and nodded. And when the arrow was released, there was no doubt from anyone on the ground that it would hit the target, and hit the target it did – right down the centre of the eye.

Drona embraced Arjuna in joy and immediately felt a special affection for the young Pandava, a sign of things to come as Arjuna would eventually become Drona's favourite disciple. Drona chided the rest of his students on their lack of focus, reminding them on the importance of unbroken focus. Citing Arjuna as his example, he reminded them of how a person should remain focussed in all circumstances despite the many distractions that may exist around them.

How Arjuna Became Drona's Favourite

Over the years Arjuna would display unfailing devotion to Drona and an eagerness to learn that pleased the grandmaster immensely. Arjuna would always be found by his teacher's side, asking questions and practising with his weapons. Drona's affection towards Arjuna grew with each passing day with admiration over his focus and diligence to improve himself. Drona even shared with Arjuna the secret of celestial weapons that he learnt from his guru Parasurama, which until then remained something that was only revealed to his son Ashwatthama.

Without the knowledge passed on to him by Drona, Arjuna would never have been the feared warrior that he was, and he became the mainstay of the Pandavas during the great war; protecting Yudhisthira and constantly wreaking havoc on the Kaurava troops. His ability to fight several warriors at the same time is wholly-attributed to Drona, so is his skilful handling of weapons while on chariots or horseback.

One of Drona's greatest failings was said to be his preference towards his personal favourites. His favouritism sometimes borders being unfair, as seen in the story of him rejecting a young Nishada, Ekalavya not once but twice, the first due to his belief in social classes. Ekalavya who had aspired to be a student of the grandmaster, was rejected with the excuse of him not being of princely stature (Ekalavya being a forest tribe leader's son).

Disconsolate but not surrendering his hopes, a determined Ekalavya proceeded to create a statue of Drona of hard wood, and continued to practise archery after worshipping this image (which he considered his guru) every day. In time, he became a peerless warrior, armed with the mission of becoming the greatest archer of all-time, completely through self-practice.

It is this same favouritism towards Arjuna that forced Drona to unfairly treat Ekalavya the second time he came across the forest dweller. During one of their usual strolls in the forest, Drona and the Pandavas came across a dog whose mouth was bound by special arrows that prevented it from barking, albeit without hurting the creature. Arjuna immediately started to fear that there was someone more skilful than him with the bow, and approached Drona, asking him, "Master, you promised to make me the greatest archer alive, but today I see a feat that I cannot even imagine accomplishing with my bow."

Confused himself over the existence of an archer with such abilities, Drona reassured Arjuna while instructing the brothers to look for any archer practising nearby. And thus, they came across Ekalavya, who immediately fell on Drona's feet saying, "Guru, it is indeed my blessing to see you again after all these years." Drona remembered his dismissal of the tribal lad all those years ago, and marvelled at the progress that Ekalavya had made over the years.

Inquiring further, Drona then discovered how Ekalavya accepted the wooden statue of him as his teacher although Ekalavya was rejected by the grandmaster. While he was amazed by Ekalavya's dexterity with the bow, he was also conscious of the promise that he had made to Arjuna and recognized the threat of having someone more skilful than his own chosen, favourite disciple.

Drona's mind started to work furiously on how he could diffuse the situation, and the solution came from Ekalavya himself who continued to prostrate himself on the ground while asking, "Please bless this devotee of yours by asking me of any guru dakshina that you desire, you have been my guru for so many years without receiving any dakshina."

Hearing this, a sudden thought crossed Drona's mind which initially felt cruel but upon further contemplation did not seem as crude as first thought. Drona justified his decision based on the fact that Ekalavya chose to continue practising archery by self-appointing his own guru, something unheard of during those times.

With an anxious Arjuna looking on, Drona requested for Ekalavya's right thumb as his dakshina, shocking even the Pandavas but not the smiling student. Ekalavya instantly unsheathed his hunting knife, slit off his right thumb and presented it to his teacher. Drona then blessed Ekalavya and left the forest with the Pandavas following closely behind, visibly in shock over what had transpired. Thus was the threat of the only known archer comparable to Arjuna effectively nullified.

Tragically, this very favouritism would eventually cause Drona's own demise as Arjuna will fight the great war on the opposite side, and together with Yudhisthira and Bhima jointly caused the death of their own teacher. It was believed that Ashwatthama also harboured ill-feeling towards Arjuna due to the favouritism that Drona constantly displayed, with repercussions of this ill-feeling seen at the end of the war.

The cousins grew up quickly, and were soon adults. Duryodhana's jealousy towards the Pandavas continued to grow as the citizens of Hastinapura openly praised the Pandavas, especially Yudhisthira whom they considered their perfect king. An angry Duryodhana would even propose to wage war against his cousins to get rid of them, but this proposition would be shot down by his father Dhritarastra, who feared the combined might of the Pandavas and their allies.

As his jealousy threatened to boil over, Duryodhana plotted to kill his cousins by sending them to Varanavata for a festival, while placing them within a palace made of combustible wax material. The Pandavas will be cryptically-forewarned by Vidura prior to their departure, and thanks to this warning and an expert miner's help, would successfully escape the trap of a burning palace via an underground tunnel.

Once safely away from Varanavata, the Pandavas and Kunti will then live as ascetics in the town of Ekachakra, where they will help the local villagers kill a man-eating demon named Bakasura.

While the denizens of Hastinapura mourned the apparent-death of the Pandavas and Kunti, the sons of Pandu will successfully participate in Draupadi's swayamwara, where Arjuna wins Draupadi's hand by winning the competition held by Panchali's father, Drupada. Due to an oath taken by the brothers to share everything between them, and also mother Kunti's order, Draupadi will be jointly-wed by all five Pandavas; though it was believed that Arjuna remained her favourite.

A Game of Dice

News of the Pandavas' re-emergence will reach Hastinapura. While the citizens were overjoyed, Duryodhana's envy would grow even further, especially now that the powerful Drupada is allied with the Pandavas. Despite Duryodhana's apparent resistance, Dhritarastra will heed the advice of elders such as Bhishma, Drona and Vidura and invite the Pandavas back to Hastinapura.

Much to Duryodhana's disbelief, the blind king would then award half of the kingdom to Yudhisthira, proclaiming him the monarch of that half. Dharmaputra will choose the ancient city of Khandavaprastha as the capital of his new empire, renaming it as Indraprastha in the process. The Pandavas, Draupadi, Kunti and the rest of the citizens of Indraprastha will then live there in harmony for more than three decades, sticking to the laws of dharma and making their kingdom wealthy and prosperous.

In time, Yudhisthira will be convinced to perform the Rajasuya ceremony by his brothers and the wise elders. He will then successfully perform this sacred sacrifice and be recognised as 'Emperor' after Bhima slew Jarasandha, arguably the only king who could have opposed the sovereignty of Dharmaputra as an emperor. At the end of the Rajasuya ceremony, Yudhisthira will take the blessings of Vyasa, who will proceed to warn the emperor of upcoming perils and destruction over the course of the next thirteen years. Heeding this warning, Yudhisthira will undertake a thirteen-year vow never to give way to anger, hostility or aggression.

Back in Hastinapura, Duryodhana was filled with burning jealousy, having just returned from Indraprastha and witnessed first-hand the prosperity enjoyed by his cousins. Unable to bear the overwhelming thoughts of their affluence, Duryodhana became absorbed in grief. Allowing evil thoughts to flood his mind, he will then succumb to temptation of the evil scheme of his uncle, Shakuni who promised to get rid of the Pandavas without waging open warfare.

Shakuni will convince the eldest Kuru prince to invite Yudhisthira for a game of dice in Hastinapura, albeit without disclosing who Dharmaputra's actual opponent was. Shakuni knew that Yudhisthira was very fond of the game, although not a very talented player. Shakuni on the other hand was well-versed with all the tricks of the game, and wanted to challenge Yudhisthira to the game with the wager being the kingdom itself. Shakuni's plan involved him eventually winning the game on behalf of Duryodhana, driving the Pandavas out of the dynasty for good.

Having successfully convinced Duryodhana, both the Kuru prince and Shakuni approached Dhritarastra for his blessings before inviting the Pandavas. Despite being resistant at first and being advised against proceeding by wise Vidura,

A Game of Dice

the blind king would eventually yield to the wishes of his son and brother-in-law to proceed with the invitation. He would then send Vidura to Indraprastha to invite Yudhisthira and the Pandavas on the pretext of witnessing the grandeur of the recently-constructed room of games, and having a fun game of dice before returning to Indraprastha.

Following the order of the king, Vidura will head to the capital of the Pandavas and relay the invitation to the son of Dharma. Although he felt a sense of reluctance in his heart, Dharmaputra could not bring himself to resist the temptation of a game of dice, and believed that it would be against the kshatriya dharma to decline the challenge of a dice game. Yudhisthira would thus gracefully accept the invitation of Dhritarastra, and on to Hastinapura did the Pandavas go, with Dharmaputra at the head of the entourage.

The rest they say, is history.

Yudhisthira would be shocked to discover that he would be playing against Shakuni instead of his cousin Duryodhana. Unable to bail himself out, fearing the label of a coward, Dharmaputra would then cast the dice against the skilful Shakuni, knowing well that he stood very little chance of winning. True enough, Yudhisthira started losing his wagers one after another. First, they played waging gold coins, then it was precious jewels and plots of land. In no time Yudhisthira had lost everything that he owned, with a smirking Shakuni seated opposite him licking his lips in further anticipation.

Unable to stop himself and praying for the tide of luck to turn, Dharmaraja would then stake his army, his palace and all his servants and citizens, and as destiny would have it – would lose all of them as well. Still Yudhisthira went on, trapped within the wretched spell of gambling, waging all his brothers one by one; starting from Sahadeva and Nakula all the way to the ever-triumphant Arjuna and mighty Bhima. Alas, as fate would have it, Yudhisthira's luck with the dice would not change and with that, he lost all his brothers.

Still unable to halt, he would then wager himself on the stake, which Shakuni would gleefully win with his next throw of the dice. Shakuni would then announce to the stunned assembly that the five Pandavas are now slaves of the Kauravas, with the likes of Bhishma, Drona, Kripa, Dhritarastra, Vidura and other elders looking on in dumbfounded-despair but helpless to do anything.

Pushing his luck further, Shakuni would then give Dharmaputra a final chance at redemption and said, "Look here Yudhisthira, I now give you the chance to regain everything that you have lost today. You have one last item in your possession that you are yet to stake, your wife Draupadi. Gamble her as your stake, and I wager all that I have won today on my side. Winner takes all. What say you?"

Visibly trembling now, but unable to resist the opportunity to win all that he had lost back in a throw of a dice, Yudhisthira received the curses of the assembly as he said, "I stake her."

The assembly's atmosphere displayed not only anxiety and agony, but also one of enhanced tension and anticipation as both Yudhisthira and Shakuni cast their dices. As fate would have it, the final round also went the way of the sneering Shakuni – and at the end of the game it became obviously clear that Yudhisthira had on that disastrous day gambled away not only all of his belongings but also catastrophically his brothers and wife.

A Game of Dice

Loud cheers were heard from the side of the Kauravas, while the rest of the assembly displayed an atmosphere of grim anticipation and apprehension, clearly uncertain of what would unfold next.

What happened next was beyond anyone's wildest imagination, and is believed to be the incident that conclusively determined the future of the Kauravas, or the lack of it.

THE INSULT OF DRAUPADI

Turning to Vidura in glee, Duryodhana said, "Bring Draupadi here! Let us have our newest servant in our presence!" Karna, ashamed by the turn of events, avoided Duryodhana's eye and moved out of the regent's sight. His dharma clearly indicated that something wrong was being committed, but just like Bhishma and Drona he chose to keep his counsel to himself and not reprimand his friend.

Vidura however had no such qualms, and responded in anger, "Duryodhana, ignorance is guiding you just as how a deer is guided into the river, not knowing the existence of the crocodile beneath it. Drunk with false ego, you are inviting death straight to your home with this action of yours. Know that the staking of Draupadi was illegal as Yudhisthira was already a slave and lost himself before staking her, thus she is not your slave as you claim."

Vidura then addressed the assembly, "Oh Dhritarastra, why do you say nothing to check this madness of your son? Bhishma, Drona and Kripa, why do you stand there with heads bowed when you see adharma transpiring right before your eyes?"

There was no response whatsoever to Vidura's questions; all the elders in the assembly remained silent as a fuming Duryodhana ignored Vidura's words and instructed his chief servant to bring Draupadi to the assembly hall. Hearing the unbelievable story of the day's occurrence in shock from the servant, Draupadi will then refuse to follow him back to the assembly hall, citing it was unlawful for one to stake someone else having first lost himself. The distressed servant returned to Duryodhana in fear, relaying what had happened at Draupadi's palace.

Fuming in anger now, Duryodhana will dismiss his chief servant and ask Karna to bring Draupadi to the hall. Karna will however bow his head in silence and not respond to Duryodhana's request. It is said that dharma will override Karna's love for his friend at that moment, and it is his adherence to dharma that will protect the king of Anga from the sin of insulting a woman.

Luckily for Karna, Duryodhana's shock at his friend's reluctance would be replaced with joy when Duhsasana proclaimed loudly, "All here are afraid of the Pandavas. Allow me to carry out this task brother, and drag Draupadi here I will if I have to!"

And that was how exactly Draupadi eventually arrived at the hall, dragged by her hair by the ruthless Duhsasana. Draupadi had first resisted, pleaded and eventually futilely attempted to flee the attention of Duhsasana, seeking refuge from anyone that would offer her sanctuary, but none appeared as the wicked son of Dhritarastra caught up with her. Catching her by the hair, Duhsasana's evil heart saw fit to humiliate the wife of the Pandavas thus, ignorant to the agony of the sobbing Panchali who was dressed in

The Insult of Draupadi

nothing but a single cloth as he brought her to the assembly hall.

Slowly rising to feet, controlling her anguish but unable to check her anger towards Yudhisthira and the assembly's elders, she asked, "I see before me countless elders learned in the Vedas and shastras. Yet an act of grief injustice was committed before you all. In your presence, you allowed the king to not only be cheated via a game of dice, but also gamble me away after he lost his own freedom. How is this dharma? Will you not respond to this gross unfairness that is happening before your eyes now?" Rebuking the likes of Bhishma, Drona and Kripa thus, Draupadi's heart fell when she realized that none responded to her admonishment, all heads were bent low in shame and guilt while Duryodhana and Duhsasana's laughter filled the court.

"No one will help you today my dear Panchali, they are loyal to the court of Hastinapura and will not refuse my wishes. Furthermore, your husband Yudhisthira lost you in the game fair and square, so there is nothing to be ashamed about now of becoming a servant in my court," Duryodhana said in jest. The Pandavas felt helpless at their inability to change the course of fate, and Bhima especially struggled with all his might to keep his temper in check.

The evil Duhsasana added, laughing, "Your husbands stand there, devoid of their royal garments as they are now slaves of this kingdom. Let me help you get unrobed and change into your new garments now, surely what you are wearing is not suitable for sweeping the floors here." A collective gasp of disbelief was heard from the assembly when everyone realized what was about to happen, though agonizingly none attempted to stop Duhsasana's wicked act.

It is said however that Dhristarastra's sons Vikarna and Yuyutsu would object to this treatment of Draupadi, only to be shot down by their brothers. Karna would turn a blind eye on the happenings, conscious of the adharma occurring before his eyes and refusing to be part of it, but unable to stop the vile act of Duhsasana for fear of hurting his friend Duryodhana.

Devoid of all mortal refuge and about to have her modesty outraged by an evil tyrant, an anguished Draupadi sought help from her last sanctuary, her closest friend Krishna, begging in her heart for deliverance from the nightmare that she was facing, "O Protector of the Universe, all that I have counted on have abandoned me. I seek shelter at your feet, deliver me from this terrible plight. You alone are my asylum, and in you alone I trust." Those were her last words as she collapsed on the floor, fainting.

A smirking Duhsasana then began disrobing the unconscious Draupadi, though the smirk was quickly wiped off his face as he found that his efforts seemed to be failing. Every cloth that he ripped off was miraculously replaced by a newer garment, covering Draupadi in entirety.

As most of the men of the assembly looked away, ashamed of the evil deed happening before their eyes, the divine miracle continued to keep Duhsasana's efforts at bay, until he finally fell on the floor himself, completely fatigued while Draupadi remained unconscious on the floor, but most-importantly, fully-clothed. A huge pile of garments lay around her, as if daring anyone else to further attempt to outrage her modesty.

Unable to bear the sight of his beloved Draupadi in such a deplorable state, Bhima will then undertake an oath that frightened even the bravest of the assembly, "Wicked Duhsasana, a shame to the Kuru dynasty you are. For what you have done today, may my soul not be liberated until I rip your heart apart and drink your blood!"

Still seething with anger, Bhima will then turn to Duryodhana and proclaim," Wretched Duryodhana, for daring to ask Draupadi to sit on your lap shamelessly, I promise to break that very thigh of yours in battle, or I will not reach the abode of my elders upon death!" These oaths of Bhima shook the assembly to life, with the sinful ones trembling in fear in the face of the mighty Pandava.

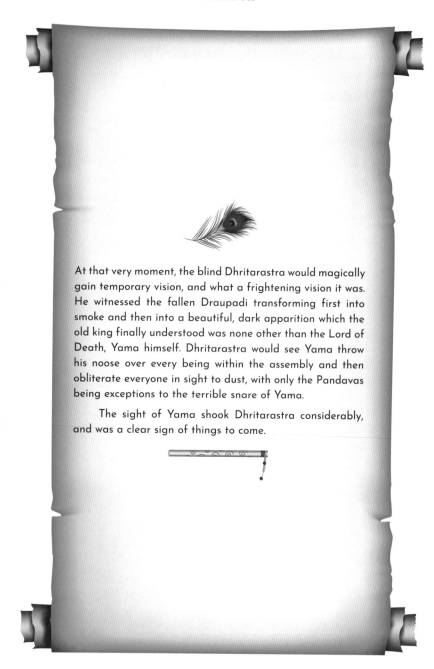

At that very moment, the blind Dhritarastra would magically gain temporary vision, and what a frightening vision it was. He witnessed the fallen Draupadi transforming first into smoke and then into a beautiful, dark apparition which the old king finally understood was none other than the Lord of Death, Yama himself. Dhritarastra would see Yama throw his noose over every being within the assembly and then obliterate everyone in sight to dust, with only the Pandavas being exceptions to the terrible snare of Yama.

The sight of Yama shook Dhritarastra considerably, and was a clear sign of things to come.

Part Two

In Exile and Beyond

The Pandavas Exiled

And with that terrible vision, Dhritarastra felt all his other senses returning to him. Finding himself unable to see again, he got to his feet and at last acted with some dignity and courage. Addressing Duryodhana, he shouted, "Stop Duryodhana. You have insulted your cousins enough! And what have you and Duhsasana done to Draupadi? Stop at once and seek their forgiveness."

He then gestured to a recovering Panchali to approach him, in an attempt to console her and correct the wrongs that had been committed. In what was to follow, much to Duryodhana's chagrin, Dhritarastra would bless Draupadi with as many boons as she wished for, and sought to fulfil all her wishes immediately.

A shell-shocked Draupadi, knowing that Dhritarastra acted upon fear as he did not object to her being humiliated by his son earlier, would first seek the freedom of Yudhisthira. With her next wish, she would ask for the freedom of the other Pandavas, with their weapons and chariots. Dhritarastra would grant both wishes without hesitance, truly afraid now of the fate of his race and sons, ignoring the enraged Duryodhana who saw his grand plan failing miserably before his eyes.

The old king would then ask Yudhisthira to come to him, and apologized profusely for the mistakes of his sons, "My dear Dharmaputra, I wish for nothing but peace between you and my sons. Please accept my apologies on behalf of my wicked sons for I only wanted you to come for a friendly game of dice and was not aware of the evil scheme that was planned. Pray, forget all that had happened today and dismiss it from your memory. Go back in peace now with your brothers, all your belongings and kingdom in-tact. Please take them all back, live in freedom and prosperity with your loved ones. Go now, son of Dharma."

Visibly stunned by the turn of events, and still in a state of shock, the Pandavas would then leave for Indraprastha with Draupadi, leaving a very noisy assembly behind. Dhritarastra would dismiss the assembly and retired to his chambers, suddenly feeling very tired. Later in the day, an enraged Duryodhana, having been provoked by Shakuni and Duhsasana, would approach his father and continued to incite hatred against the Pandavas, citing the obvious strength of his cousins that needed to be checked.

The weak-willed Dhritarastra always had a soft spot for Duryodhana, and as always could not say no to his favourite son. He was also tempted by the possibility of the Kauravas finally becoming the ultimate rulers of the land if they got rid of the Pandavas, as he was tired of living in the shadows of first his brother Pandu and now Pandu's offspring.

As a result, the blind king would go back on his word and agreed to a last game of dice between the Pandavas and Kauravas, within which everything was to be settled. Despite the objections of the other Kuru elders, Dhritarastra sent an emissary to Indraprastha to invite the Pandavas again, knowing that proud kshatriyas would not allow themselves to decline a challenge to a game of dice.

As destiny would have it, Yudhisthira would be enticed once again by the invite and true to the code of kshatriyas, would accept the challenge. Bhagavan Vyasa would compare this acceptance of inevitability on the part of Yudhisthira to how Shri Rama would go in pursuit of the golden deer in Treta Yuga, although the king of Ayodhya knew well enough that in reality, a golden deer simply did not exist. No one could defeat destiny, be it good or evil, as the path that must be trodden has been fixed and everything else are merely tools in the ploy of the Supreme.

Once he reached Hastinapura for the second time in the day, Dharmaputra found Shakuni waiting with the game of dice, willing the intended destiny to unfold. The elders of the assembly tried in vain to stop Yudhisthira from casting the dice, to no avail.

The stake was set this time, the losing party was to be banished to the forest for a full twelve years before spending a thirteenth year in hiding, not to be discovered. If the defeated party was recognized during that year, they would need to serve another twelve years in the forest in exile. The defeated party would however obtain their share of the kingdom once they successfully return from exile.

Knowing that he had very little chance of success, Yudhisthira had resigned himself to defeat even before he threw the dice. Once the dice were cast by both parties, his worst fears were realized, he had lost.

And as ordained, the Pandavas and Draupadi would change their garments to those of tree bark and deerskin, suitable for their upcoming life as ascetics, and discarded their royal garments that are of little use to them. Not wanting to spend any more time in the wretched hall, the Pandavas then hastily left Hastinapura, accompanied by the tears of the elders such as Bhishma, Drona and Vidura.

Duhsasana and Duryodhana will continue to taunt their cousins as they made their way out. The taunting reached a point when Bhima will not be able to take it any longer and exclaimed loudly, "Hear us now citizens of Hastinapura. We may be exiled now but we will be back to regain what we have lost. We know that Duryodhana will not return the kingdom to us, thus war will be certain. I will personally kill Duryodhana, Duhsasana and all their evil brothers. Arjuna will kill Karna, Sahadeva will kill Shakuni, and Nakula will kill the sons of Duryodhana." Having said thus, Bhima followed Yudhisthira and the rest into the forest, with the spirit of revenge scorching brightly inside him.

The Pandavas Exiled

Truly fate spares no one. From being a glorious emperor, Yudhisthira has now been reduced to having to adorn the garbs of an ascetic, with 13 years in the wilderness ahead of him. Before leaving for the forest, Dharmaputra will ask uncle Vidura to look after their mother Kunti while they were away in exile, something that Vidura would gladly agree to.

The citizens would be heartbroken to see the beloved Pandavas leave, and within their lamentations would also curse the Kuru elders for the inaction in allowing the unthinkable to happen. Evil omens will be seen as the Pandavas left Hastinapura on foot, with jackals howling at odd hours and the sky turning into a glum, dark grey colour; the sun nowhere to be seen. All of these signs further increased Dhritarastra's anxiety, but the blind king did not attempt to reconcile with the Pandavas, for he knew that things had gone too far this time.

The Pandavas and Draupadi would move from place to place, visiting hermitages of renowned sages and receiving their blessings while they counted their days until the first twelve years elapsed. Krishna will also visit his dear friends in the forest, and took time to console a weeping Draupadi, assuring her that the Pandavas will undoubtedly regain their lost kingdom in good time, as they have been steadfast in their dharma and never have they wished ill of others.

The years sauntered by, and the brothers spent their time practicing archery and sparring with each other with the mace, while also obtaining more Vedic and spiritual knowledge from the sages they visited. Yudhisthira constantly struggled to keep the tempers of both Bhima and Arjuna in check during these years, as both carried with them a strong will to physically right the wrong and win back their kingdom upon their return.

The time then arrived for Yudhisthira to share with Arjuna Bhagavan Vyasa's instructions - to ensure that Partha obtains the knowledge of the celestial weapon of the gods, without which they will be hopelessly overpowered against the combined might of Bhishma, Drona, Kripa, Ashwatthama and Karna in any upcoming war. So on went Arjuna to the Himalayas, held by a steely resolve and armed with knowledge of the Pratismriti mantra endowed by Vyasa, one that allowed him to reach the Himalayas within the same day.

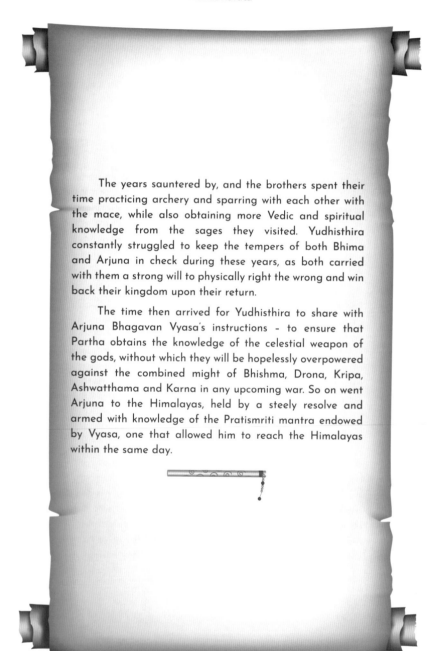

Arjuna Obtains Celestial Weapons

Clad in full armour with the Gandiva in hand, Arjuna started his journey up the Himalayas, eager to attain his father Indra's blessings and hopefully, the rest of the gods as well. With thoughts of his brothers and Draupadi firmly behind him, Arjuna eventually reached the famed Indrakeeladri Hill, which he climbed to high enough a plateau to have a fantastic bird-eye view of surrounding areas. While exploring the highlands, Arjuna came across an ascetic under an ancient tree, seated in meditating position.

Arjuna approached the brahmana, who sensed Arjuna's presence, slowly opened his eyes and said, "Who are you warrior? There is no place for kshatriyas up here, nor for the weapons that they carry. Know that this is the abode for those that have conquered their senses, and do not seek worldly joys anymore. Considering that you have actually made it this far, you must be filled with purity, as such throw away your weapons and join me in perfecting your life."

Studying the magnificent-looking brahmin carefully, Arjuna understood that he was no ordinary sage. Arjuna however remained steadfast in his mission, and replied, "Oh sage, I bow to you, ask me for anything but to throw away my arms. I need them to right the wrongs that have been dealt onto my brothers and I. Please bless me with the presence of Indra for I desire for celestial weapons as well."

Thoroughly happy with Arjuna's sense of duty and dedication towards his dharma, the sage then disclosed his true self, "Pleased am I with your response Dhananjaya. Know that I am Indra, the very one that you seek. Your wish for celestial weapons is understood, but why wish for such petty matters when I can bless you with immortality and bliss in the higher regions of the gods? Ask for that and I would happily grant it immediately!"

Arjuna's reply to his father was respectful but firm, "Blessed am I to have the vision of the king of the gods. O father, I have very little wish for the pleasure of the higher regions at the moment. What I need is the knowledge of all your weapons, and to return to my brothers and Draupadi, whom I have sworn to protect with my life."

Indra's admiration for his son grew, but he wanted to put Partha through one last trial, thus he said, "O Arjuna, I would be pleased to bless you with all the weapons I own, however, you will have earned this knowledge only after satisfying Shiva, the three-eyed God."

Having said thus, Indra disappeared from sight, leaving Arjuna bewildered on how he could receive Shivas grace. Indra's intention was to not only ensure that his son would have the blessing of Shiva, but also so that Partha might be fortunate enough to be awarded Shiva's own Pashupathi-astra; an astra so devastating that it could challenge even the Brahma-astra in destruction force.

Arjuna Obtains Celestial Weapons

Arjuna decided to return to the ancient tree where he found Indra, and discarding all his weapons went into deep meditation. Blocking off all external thoughts and sensations, Arjuna focussed his mind completely on Shiva, and only returned to consciousness to sustain his physical body, that too by eating just fruits. By the end of the month Arjuna ignored even that, surviving purely on the power of meditation, forsaking all physical requirements.

As days went by Arjuna's exploits started to display unmistakable signs; an eternally-glowing new physique was seen on the warrior, while the earth he stood on started to burn and smoke was seen emitting from his body. As the intensity of his penances increased, the gods and rishis started feeling distressed, fearing for the safety of the Himalayas which had started to tremble with the sheer strength of Partha's austerities. They jointly approached Shiva, who reassured them that he was fully-aware of Arjuna's wishes and would in due time fulfil the warrior's wishes.

Shiva then transformed into his favourite human form, the hunter, and descended from his abode to where Arjuna was. As he approached Partha, he noticed a demonic wild boar, visibly disturbed by the smoke emanating from Arjuna's body and about to charge at the Pandava. At the same time, the Pandava heard the bellows of the boar, immediately springing into action – stringing the Gandiva, attaching a bow to it before releasing the arrow.

Unknown to him however, Shiva already had the boar in his sight, and knowing it to be a demon in disguise trying to disturb Arjuna's meditation, had released his very own arrow at exactly the same moment as the Pandava. The boar stood no chance, transforming back to its demon form and instantly falling down dead. No demon could survive being hit by two arrows from not only the Gandiva but also Shiva's very own Pinaka.

Arjuna moved his attention to the hunter, not missing the obvious gleam emitting from the well-built body of the man, seemingly brightening up the mountains itself with his shimmering presence. He was nonetheless furious that another man had shot at the animal that he had aimed for, and shouted at the hunter, "Who are you hunter? How dare you shoot at the very beast that I had in my sight already and successfully brought down? Do you not know that aiming for the target of another is against the very laws of hunting in the forest?"

In response to Arjuna, the hunter merely sniggered in apparent irritation, "Stop living in the imagination that you killed the beast with your arrow. You look like an ascetic who accidentally learnt to use the bow along the way. The very bow that you hold seems too big for your small physique, best let it rest before you hurt yourself with it. It was without doubt my arrow that pierced the boar, and I am happy to prove you wrong if you still believed differently."

Responding to the hunter's taunt, Arjuna sprang into action, picking up the Gandiva and showering immeasurable arrows on the hunter. But alas, the normally-deadly Gandiva appeared to have lost its prowess on the hunter as the arrows bounced off his body like toy arrows, leaving Arjuna utterly amazed.

Not losing heart, the Pandava continued showering sharper and stronger arrows on his opponent, but he was stunned to discover that none of his arrows pierced his adversary in the slightest. He was then further astounded to find his inexhaustible magical quiver empty; a scenario not even he could have imagined! With a smile, the hunter then took out an arrow of his own, and within one swift movement fixed and released his arrow, disarming a shell-shocked Arjuna of the Gandiva before saying, "Is that all you have to offer?"

In shock but driven by anger and determination, Arjuna took up a mace and pounced on his rival. Now laughing, the hunter simply caught hold of the mace, effortlessly wrestled it out of the Pandava's hand and threw it away, out of reach. Starting to feel disgraced of being bullied into submission by someone seemingly-nothing more than an ordinary hunter, Arjuna did not lose heart but drew his sword and re-started the battle. Striking his opponent on his right arm, Arjuna was filled with utmost astonishment when he found his sword reduced to smithereens the moment it struck the frame of the hunter.

Doubt started to creep into his mind of who the hunter really was, but dispelling his misgivings and wanting to cause hurt to his opponent in any way possible, Arjuna started to rain punches on his opponent using his bare fists, eventually attempting to wrestle the hunter to the ground. To his utter amazement and humiliation, his rival pulled him into a bear lock so tight that Arjuna found himself struggling to breathe, eventually submitting to defeat. When the hunter finally released him, Arjuna found his foe unable to stop laughing at the Pandava's futile efforts, and within his own embarrassment and fast-disappearing ego Arjuna's mind began to clear.

Reality finally dawned upon Arjuna when he realized that this must be the greatest of gods, the blue-throated Shiva. None other than Mahadeva can withstand such arrows and blows and still stand there laughing, unperturbed at the very least. Falling to the ground in obeisance, Arjuna apologized to Shiva and begged for his forgiveness for daring to challenge him to a duel.

Smiling broadly now, Shiva brought Arjuna back to his feet before embracing him, the Pandava finding his battered condition returning to perfection simply by the divine touch of Shiva. Shiva's embrace would also transform Arjuna's strength to a hundred times more than before, and the three-eyed god would then reward Arjuna with the divine Pashupathi-astra, the knowledge of which was unknown even to the gods such as Indra or Kubera. Blessing Partha with unfailing success, Shiva would then disappear from sight leaving Arjuna complete awed, overcome by gratitude for his good fortune of being graced by the presence of Mahadeva.

Indra would then take Arjuna to his abode, and as promised will teach his son the knowledge of drawing and withdrawing all the celestial weapons within his arsenal, starting with his very own Vajra and Indra-astra. After Indra, the other protective gods followed suit, starting with Dharma who blessed Arjuna with the utilization of his celestial mace. This was followed by Varuna who awarded the Pandava with the Nagapasha noose, before finally Kubera who would teach Partha of the use of his very-own mace, the Antardhana.

The Lokapalas would then bless the warrior with long life and certain success in all future battles before bidding him goodbye. Arjuna would be left to thank his lucky stars as he had successfully fulfilled his mission to obtain celestial weapons, and would be taken back to the realm of mortals by Indra's charioteer, Mataali where he would be reunited with his joyful brothers and Panchali.

While Arjuna successfully obtained celestial weapons after his blessed encounter with the three-eyed Mahadeva and the protective Lokapalas before reuniting with the rest of his brothers and Draupadi, his elder brother Bhima would have his very own divine encounter a few months later.

BHIMA MEETS HANUMAN

One beautiful day during their exile in the forest, Draupadi and the Pandavas were having their morning stroll when a gorgeous flower made its way to Panchali, enchanting her not only with its appearance but more potently its ultra-sweet fragrance, making her fall in love with the flower at once. She excitedly showed the flower off to Bhima who was closest to her and exclaimed, "See Bhima, such a beautiful flower and how delightfully fragrant it is. Let's find its source and plant the flower near our cottage so that we can smell its sweet fragrance every morning!"

Ever-eager to make his beloved Draupadi happy, Bhima quickly took leave of the others and followed the fragrance of the plant, seemingly brought by the breeze of the moment. Without carrying any weapon or fear of any wild beast, Bhima continued his journey which took him deep into the forest before he chanced upon the very plant that he was looking for.

Located within a strange-looking garden within a large clearing beneath a mountain, it was clear how the breeze carried the flower's fragrance all the way to where the

Pandavas were earlier, as it was the biggest garden of flowers Bhima had ever seen. Even stranger however, was the sight of a giant monkey blocking his path to the garden where the flowers grew.

Eager to return to Draupadi and his brothers, Bhima started a slow run towards the garden, but found that the only path into the garden was blocked by the large monkey. Shouting and howling to scare the monkey away, Bhima found an uninterested creature that merely half-opened its eyes and closed them again. Becoming agitated now, Bhima then poked the monkey on its back, asking it to move out of the way.

To which the monkey replied, "O giant human, why do you torture an old monkey in such a manner? You look like a learned human being who should be well-versed in the manner of treating inferior beings, so why do you treat me such, forgetting all that you have learnt? Do show me the mercy that I deserve as an old, dispensable monkey."

The monkey added further, "However, if you are seeking to go down this path, I will have to disappoint you as the path that you seek is limited only to gods and celestial beings, and out-of-bounds to humans such as yourself. You are however permitted to eat the fruits around this area around you and then head back in peace, but do not seek to go further."

Listening to these words from a creature that he had very little respect for, Bhima grew angry and bellowed, "Old monkey, who are you and why do you block my path? Know that I am Bhima, son of Vaayu the Wind God and one of the world-renowned Pandavas. Your small talk does not interest me, on the other hand I fully intend to go down this path to obtain those flowers that I see as my Draupadi has requested for them. Once I have obtained them, I will head back in peace, but if you block my path, I will have no other option but to forcibly remove you before entering the garden. Move away now before I make minced meat out of you!"

Hardly-perturbed without looking the least interested, the monkey replied, "Do not say that I did not warn you. I may be an old monkey, but at least I know my manners and appreciate good advice when I hear them. At your peril then."

Completely losing his patience now, Bhima cried, "I don't need advice from an old monkey on what I can or cannot do. This is your last chance, move out of the way or you will feel Bhima's fist!"

The monkey merely smiled and replied again, "Dear warrior, being a very old monkey, I have lost the energy to stand or move on my own. Why don't you spare me the effort and jump over me? You should be gentle to the weak as you are strong and young, so spare this old monkey some mercy and don't make me move from my resting place." Bhima scoffed at this suggestion and said, "O monkey, if only the scriptures allowed it, I would have jumped over you in an instant similar to how valiant Hanuman jumped across the ocean."

Feigning surprise, the monkey probed, "This Hanuman you speak of seems like a very interesting character, could you tell me more of his story? To which Bhima replied, "Learn from me that Hanuman is my elder brother, the bravest of the Vaanara tribe, son of Vaayu, and Lord Rama's most beloved devotee. During the mission to seek and find Lord Rama's wife Sita who was abducted by Lanka's ruler Raavana, he jumped across the ocean and successfully not only found

Sita but also burnt down part of Raavana's kingdom which until then was impregnable. Know that I am as strong as my brother Hanuman, so stop this idle talk and move away from my path to the flowers!"

Smiling slightly now, the monkey replied, "As you are not allowed to jump over me, please do me a favour and move this old monkey away from your path by pushing my tail aside, which would allow you a path into the garden." Wasting no further time, and proudly confident of his immense strength, Bhima immediately pounced upon the monkey's tail with the idea of yanking the creature out of the way. To his utter horror and amazement however, he found that not only did he fail to carry the tail, he was not able to even move it an inch!

Collecting all his strength, Bhima tried time and again but still failed; the tail did not budge at all. Still he did not give up, straining so much until his muscles started to ache and he was completely covered in perspiration. Still he failed to move the tail even a little, until he was finally filled with shame and embarrassment and with a bowed head, asked for forgiveness from the old monkey, "You are definitely no ordinary being, please forgive my harsh character and reveal to me who you really are. I bow in front of you having exhausted all of my strength, and pray that you disclose who you really are."

Fully-smiling now, the monkey stood up to display its full radiant form before addressing Bhima, "O Bhima, know that I am the very same Hanuman that you spoke about a moment ago, the exact same Vaanara that lived a life blessed by the presence of his Lord Rama and Mother Sita, and who is now blessed again to be able to meet his younger brother, the pride of the Pandavas. I am joyful beyond words to finally be able to meet you in flesh my brother."

Hanuman continued, "This path that you seek to go beyond is part of the celestial world, and is filled with rakshasas that would cause you mortal danger, hence I did not allow you to go through. The original plants that you seek grow within Kubera's garden at the foot of Gandhamadhana Hill which is visible from here, but they are guarded by the celestial rakshasas Maniman and Krodhavasha, hence it will not be possible for you to collect them from that garden. I am however fully aware of what you came for, and you will find the very same Saugandhika flower plant along a stream close by, let me show you where."

Hearing the words of Hanuman, an utterly-delighted Bhima embraced Hanuman and replied, "What a blessing it is to be able to meet my brother, I count myself the most blessed of humans alive! And if it is not too much to ask, can you bless your brother with a vision of your form that crossed the ocean all those years ago?"

A smiling Hanuman proceeded to expand his size until he appeared mountain-like before an amazed Bhima who had to eventually close his eyes, the dazzling light emanating from Hanuman becoming too much for his eyes to bear. When Bhima re-opened his eyes, Hanuman was back to his original form and once again embraced Bhima, an embrace that was said to have increased Bhima's strength by many-folds as Hanuman transferred a portion of his supernatural strength to his brother.

Hanuman then proceeded to bring Bhima to the Saugandhika plant, and Bhima collected some flowers and a few branches of the plant to re-plant close to their cottage.

As a blessing before they parted, Hanuman promised Bhima this, "Whenever you raise your battle roar on the battlefield, be assured that my voice will join yours and together we shall make the enemies quake in fear. Think of me whenever you face any fear, and that fear will be dispelled immediately. I will also be present on your brother Arjuna's flag, victory will definitely be with you and your brothers. I felt the same joy embracing you as I felt when I embraced the body of my Lord Rama all those years ago, which means that you are blessed with the presence of the divine just as I was during the glorious years I spent with my living god."

Little did Bhima know that Hanuman was actually referring to Krishna, who would eventually guide the Pandavas throughout the war and beyond, and would remain their dearest friend till the end.

Remembering Draupadi and his brothers, Bhima then embraced Hanuman one last time and hurried back with the promised flowers, eager to see his Draupadi smile in joy when he returns having fulfilled her wish.

Thus did the twelve years in the forest end, and the Pandavas will spend the final year of their exile incognito within the Matsya kingdom of Virata, with each of the Pandavas and Draupadi disguising themselves as commoners and finding employment within Virata's palace. The year will pass by quickly, and culminated in a battle to defend Matsya from the Kauravas in which Arjuna will single-handedly defeat all the Kaurava maharathas in battle.

Having completed the stipulated 13 years in exile, the Pandavas then settled in Upaplavya as they decided on their next steps. Balarama, Krishna, Satyaki, Drupada, Dhristadyumna, Sikhandin and many other warriors aligned with the Pandavas joined them, and after much deliberation all agreed to approach the Kauravas peacefully, requesting for the return of half the kingdom.

It was decided to dispatch a group of brahmanas to Hastinapura and negotiate with the Kauravas as representatives of the Pandavas, despite the slim chance of peace being obtained. The kings and warriors then returned to their respective kingdoms, leaving the Pandavas to start preparations for war, in case their peace efforts proved to be futile.

With Krishna back in his capital Dwaraka, both Arjuna and Duryodhana approached Krishna's city with the hope of having Madhava and the formidable Yadava tribe on their side if battle commenced.

How Krishna Became Arjuna's Charioteer

Hearing that Krishna was back in his kingdom, Duryodhana wasted very little time and sped to Dwaraka in his chariot, not stopping to rest until he arrived at Krishna's palace. Likewise, the Pandavas were also gathering their troops, and to obtain Krishna's allegiance, Yudhisthira decided to send Arjuna himself to Dwaraka. By the turn of fate both Duryodhana and Arjuna would arrive at exactly the same moment, and rushed towards Krishna's inner chamber to meet Madhava first, fully-understanding the intention of the other.

By chance Duryodhana entered the chamber first, and finding Krishna to be fast asleep, found a seat next to the head of the bed and placed himself there, waiting for Madhava to wake up. Arjuna on the other hand stood at the foot of the bed, and patiently waited for Krishna to emerge from his slumber. After some time, Krishna opened his eyes and immediately saw Arjuna standing close to his feet, and greeted him with joy. He was further surprised to find Duryodhana seated in the same room, turning to him and warmly welcoming the eldest son of Dhritarastra. After the welcomes were over, Krishna sat with both princes, enquiring the intention of their visits.

Duryodhana spoke first, "O Janardhana, I will come straight to the point. It looks like war is upon us, and the Kauravas seek your support and guidance in this upcoming battle. Knowing that both the Kauravas and Pandavas are equally affectionate to you, I arrived her first before Arjuna and as per our scriptures decree, should be given preference. Do not go against dharma, as tradition has shown that the first to arrive is always given the first choice."

Krishna merely smiled before turning to Arjuna and asking, "What about you Partha, what can I do for you?" Arjuna bowed to Krishna in obeisance before replying, "Dear Krishna, my intention is no different to cousin Duryodhana's. With war almost certainly upon us, my only wishes are to obtain your blessings and your presence by my side during the imminent battle. There is nothing else that I desire." Krishna's smile grew wider as he considered the tricky situation that has unfolded in front of him.

On one side he had Arjuna, dearer to him than even his own sons, and also husband to his sister Subhadra. On the other side he had Duryodhana, who clearly arrived before Arjuna and is adamant of that fact. Krishna carefully contemplated of a way to navigate around the situation, keeping in mind that he had to remain unbiassed to both parties while adhering to dharma, as already highlighted by Duryodhana who clearly suspected of Krishna's impartiality towards Arjuna.

Krishna's then responded addressing the son of Dhritarastra first, "Duryodhana, while it is correct that you arrived first, but it was not you that I saw first upon waking up but Arjuna who stood waiting at my feet awaiting my awakening from slumber. As such your claim of reaching my chamber first had been equalized by my sighting of Arjuna before you, so I am bound by the scriptures to equally provide assistance to both the Pandavas and Kauravas in any conflict."

Moving on to Arjuna, Krishna continued, "Having said that, in-line with what our scriptures say, the presentation of favours start from not the eldest but the youngest of recipients. Keeping this in mind, you Arjuna will have the choice to make now as I will present you with two options. The first option will be the company of my formidable tribe; the Yadavas. They are equal in combat to even Indra's own heavenly army, and I have close to a million of these soldiers that I call my own Narayanas. The second option is having only me alone. But do consider the fact that I have decided not to take up arms in the upcoming war, though I will assist in any other possible manner with the exception of wielding a weapon. Choose wisely now Partha."

To this, Arjuna responded without a moment of hesitancy, "Gladly I choose you Krishna, I desire nothing else nor will my heart allow any other choice." Duryodhana, beaming at what he felt was foolishness on the part of Arjuna, formally requested for Krishna's tribe to be part of his army, a wish that was granted by Krishna immediately. With a spring in his step, Duryodhana took leave of both Krishna and Arjuna, pleased with the way things had turned out and laughing secretly in his heart at Arjuna's apparent idiocy.

On his way back Duryodhana stopped to meet his well-wisher Balarama. He relayed the story of what had happened with Krishna and Arjuna to Balarama, and the elder brother of Krishna would be crestfallen at the turn of events. The mighty Baladeva could not bring himself to show favouritism to either the Kauravas or Pandavas, nor could he imagine himself fighting a war on the opposite side of his brother Krishna. At the end the great Balarama will take no part in the upcoming war, choosing instead to go on pilgrimage and returning only after the great war had reached its conclusion.

As history would have it, Krishna would eventually become Arjuna's charioteer, earning the immortal name Parthasarathy (Partha's charioteer) in the process. Together Krishna and Arjuna would cause mayhem in the Kauravas' forces and be the single most prominent factor in determining the course of the war.

Preparations for war were well-underway. As both the Pandavas and Kauravas started gathering their troops, things start to move very quickly. The uncle of the Pandavas and brother of Madri, King Salya will be tricked by Duryodhana into serving the Kauravas during the war. The group of brahmanas dispatched from Drupada's court arrived in Hastinapura with the hope avoiding war, and relayed the message from the Pandavas to Dhritarastra.

As a response, Dhritarastra will send his personal assistant Sanjaya to meet the Pandavas on a peace mission, stopping short however of promising to return their kingdom. Yudhisthira will gladly welcome Sanjaya, and understanding the purpose of Sanjaya's mission, will seek Krishna's counsel on the best way to proceed. Krishna will decide to head to Hastinapura himself to negotiate the terms of a peaceful settlement and avoid war at all costs, unless it becomes unavoidable.

Before sending Sanjaya back to Hastinapura, Yudhisthira will request for at the very minimum five villages for the Pandavas, citing that peace is foremost on his mind. Back in Hastinapura, Bhishma, Vidura, Drona and Kripa will advise Dhritarastra to return half of the kingdom to the sons of Pandu, and against going to war with them, something that the blind king will wholeheartedly agree with. But as usual, he would be powerless against the foolish wishes of his son Duryodhana who refused to return not even an inch of land back to the Pandavas.

Back at Upaplavya, Krishna sought the opinions of all the brothers before leaving for Hastinapura, and was pleasantly shocked to discover that even the quick-tempered Bhima and battle-ready Arjuna sought to achieve peace rather than war, though they harboured very little hope of actually regaining their kingdom peacefully.

The last person he met before leaving the assembly was a tearful Draupadi, who reminded him of her anguish and humiliation at Dhritarastra's court. To which Krishna responded, "Worry not Krishnaa, despite the mission that I now undertake to achieve peace, I have no doubt whatsoever that the evil Duryodhana will not heed my advice and war will be upon us in no time. Mark my words, the Pandavas will annihilate the Kauravas in battle, and you will be avenged. This is destiny as the gods have ordained, and you shall live to see it happen." Hearing these words, Draupadi was pacified.

Back in Hastinapura, lamenting his fate and the foolishness of his ill-advised son, Dhritarastra placed his hopes on Krishna's imminent arrival to possibly knock some sense into his son's stubborn head, truly fearing for the future of his race now.

KRISHNA ADVOCATES PEACE

Before dawn broke the next morning, Krishna's chariot was seen blazing towards Hastinapura with Madhava and Satyaki in tow. In Hastinapura he expected a true test of his persuasion and negotiation skills in an assembly filled with not only the likes of Dhritarastra, Bhishma and Drona but more-damagingly to his mission, Duryodhana, Shakuni and Duhsasana. At Krishna's intended-destination, much to the consternation of the court elders, Duryodhana had devised with Shakuni a wicked plan to take Krishna captive as soon as he arrived at the assembly.

When Krishna finally arrived in Hastinapura, he was brought without any delay to Dhritarastra's court, where the old king and Duryodhana received Madhava with the traditional respect reserved for the most important of guests. As it was almost nightfall, it was decided that Krishna was to rest for the night before meeting a full assembly at Dhritarastra's royal court the next morning. Despite Duryodhana's offer of an opulent palace for the night's rest, Krishna's chose to accept the hospitality of Vidura's humble home instead, citing that it was not right for a messenger to accept luxurious hospitality from his host before successfully completing his mission.

Krishna would spend some time with Vidura and Kunti, having dinner with them before taking his leave and retiring for the night. The next morning, Krishna would jump into his chariot and encouraged Daruka to speed towards Dhritarastra's court, eager to complete his mission. The whole court buzzed in excited anticipation as Krishna's chariot was heard entering the compounds of the palace, and in no time Krishna himself was sighted walking into the hall, Vidura and Satyaki loyally walking alongside him.

At this sight all in the hall rose in respect, and Krishna acknowledged Dhritarastra, Bhishma, Drona, Kripa and the rest of the Kuru elders before taking his seat. He was then received with full honours by all that were present, and by the time Krishna rose to speak the whole hall had already assumed an atmosphere of serenity and silence.

Looking directly at Dhritarastra, Krishna said without hesitance, "Pleased am I to see the entire race of Kuru assembled here today, as I have come here to achieve nothing but peace between the Kauravas and the Pandavas. As the current king of the monarchy, I hold you responsible towards the future of your race. As part of the famed Kuru dynasty, you come from a line of virtuous, noble kings, and I know that you are no different from your ancestors."

Without pausing, Madhava continued, "Wise Dhritarastra, a calamity is at your door today, but only if you remain stubbornly on the wrong path. Take heed of your ancestors and make the right call; let righteousness, truthfulness and compassion be your guide, and choose peace over war. Your sons have been ill-advised and have

Krishna Advocates Peace

followed the path of adharma for ages now, the time is high for you to check them once and for all and revert them back to the path of dharma. Remember, there are no winners in a war, only death and anguish will accompany you at the end of every war."

Krishna then added, "The Pandavas are sons of your brother, and as such as your sons as well. They have been punished enough, suffering thirteen years in exile, and now seek the return of their kingdom as rightfully so."

Seeing wisdom in Krishna's words, Dhritarastra responded weakly, "Dear Madhava, I know that you speak nothing but the truth, and wish for the wellbeing of the Kauravas as much as the Pandavas. But I am helpless in convincing my son who constantly overrides my desire for peace. Pray, try to convince him against war with the elders present today, I truly wish that he will be swayed towards the path of truth."

Understanding that the decision is truly out of the old king's hand, Krishna turned to Duryodhana and said, "Duryodhana, you have heard your father's wishes for peace, and know that I wish for nothing but prosperity and happiness for you. Treat your cousins the way you would treat your brothers, and return half the kingdom to them. Leave aside all hatred and resentments towards them, as these are evil traits that will bring nothing but ruin for your entire race. Make peace and make your father happy, as this is his wish."

Seeing an impassive Duryodhana failing to respond to Krishna, Bhishma and Drona both echoed Krishna's sentiments and attempted to convince the Kuru prince of avoiding war. Vidura chipped in as well, before Dhritarastra pleaded with his son to accept Krishna's advice and forego war in view of peace with the Pandavas.

Tired of words encouraging peace and none speaking of the welfare of the Kauravas, a livid Duryodhana exploded, "O Krishna, why do you criticize me when the one who lost his kingdom is the eldest of the Pandavas, Yudhisthira himself? Nobody forced him to play, he played at his own free will and lost everything he owned. He could have stopped as he pleased but he chose to stake his belongings one after another, losing them all. Why do you not blame him then Madhava?"

Still in anger, Duryodhana continued, "The Pandavas have lawfully lost all possession of their kingdom, and it now belongs to the Kauravas. I will not return it to them. Even when I was younger and my father was the right heir to the kingdom, his younger brother Pandu was wrongly made king even while my father was alive. Pandu's son then continued as if he was the rightful king when I am the legal heir to the kingdom as son of the Dhritarastra, the rightful king. The wrongs of the past have now been rightfully corrected, and I see no need to return any kingdom to anyone."

Seeing that Dhritarastra remained silent at his son's outburst, Krishna turned stern and replied, "Take this as your final warning Duryodhana. Repent now. If you do not agree to peacefully return half the kingdom or at the very least five villages to your cousins, they will be forced to take back what belongs to them in battle." To which Duryodhana angrily declared, "Hear my decision Krishna, while I am alive, I will not give back even a needle point of land to the Pandavas!"

Shaking his head in disappointment, Krishna will then rebuke Dhritarastra for failing to control his son, but the old king will only bow his head in shame. As a final attempt, Dhritarastra will ask his wife Gandhari to attempt to convince Duryodhana, as the wise queen is known to have a degree of control over her sons and is admired for being far-sighted. However not even Gandhari's sensible motherly advice could sway obstinate Duryodhana, and he would storm out of the hall in anger, followed by his brothers and Karna.

Once outside, Duryodhana planned with Duhsasana and Shakuni to make good his plot to capture Krishna, although Karna would highlight his reservations over the idea. Dhritarastra would then summon Duryodhana as he tried once again to convince his son, but to no avail. With all peace avenues fatigued and realizing that his mission did not achieve the desirable result, Krishna would then take leave of the elders before rising to leave the hall. In an act of obvious foolishness, Duryodhana and his retinue will then attempt to seize Madhava by force, planning to imprison him after capture.

Laughing at this futile attempt at his life, Krishna will then disclose his divinity, transforming into his original four-handed form and blinding everyone around him into helpless submission. Apart from a chosen handful, Duryodhana and the rest of the assembly would fall into unconsciousness, only recovering long after Krishna had left the hall, living to regret their idiocy in attempting to capture and imprison divinity himself.

It is said that only Bhishma, Drona, Kripa, Vidura and Sanjaya were able to keep their eyes open for a view of Krishna in his universal form, a reward for living a life filled with austerities and in accordance dharma. Krishna will also bless the blind Dhritarastra with temporary vision so that the old king could see Madhava for what he really was. Having witnessed Krishna in his transcendental form, an awe-filled Dhritarastra would count himself blessed for eternity, and would wish to be blind again, with no desire to see anything else.

War was now not a possibility anymore, but an absolute certainty.

A Mother's Dilemma

Krishna left the assembly of elders and on his way home, stopped to visit Kunti at her quarters within the palace. He relayed the story of his failed mission to her, and she listened without blinking until tears started to fill her eyes as she contemplated the future war that will shortly be upon them.

Before Krishna left, Kunti uttered in a stuttering voice, "O Govinda, it is now time for the world to be devoid of all the evil that has been badgering it for decades. I bring forth my sons in this mission to cleanse the earth of its evil, and I beg of you to protect them from danger and help them achieve the missions that they have been born for."

To which Krishna replied, "Blessed mother, your sons have always followed the path of dharma, and as such no harm will come to them, and they shall definitely emerge victorious from this holy war. Fear not, as the gods themselves have blessed your sons and are always on the side of those that align with dharma."

Having said thus, Krishna jumped onto his chariot and left Hastinapura without further delay. With a mix of fear and unease in her heavy heart, Kunti watched the chariot leave the palace grounds until even the specks of dust disappeared from sight. Nevertheless, at the same time she could not help experiencing a sense of assurance knowing that Krishna will be guiding her sons throughout the upcoming ill-fated war.

Upon Krishna's departure from Hastinapura, having failed in his peace mission to avoid war, the Kaurava elders started immediate preparations for the war. Seeing the scenes of seemingly-unavoidable utter destruction folding in front of her eyes, Kunti found herself again overcome by sorrow and grief.

After a while, she gathered her strength and thought to herself, "While I cannot ask my sons to give up their birth rights and the kingdom that is rightfully theirs, going to war with their very own cousins is also something utterly dreadful, with only complete annihilation and devastation up ahead. Even if I can convince peace-loving Yudhisthira to give up the kingdom, neither will Duryodhana allow us to live in peace nor will I be able to keep the anger of Bhima, Arjuna or Draupadi in check. No joy or happiness can be obtained from killings in a war, and this war is set to destroy all that we have built so far. I am torn between upholding the honour of kshatriya's and complete annihilation; what will I do?"

Continuing to lament, overwhelmed with negative doubts, Kunti thought to herself, "Even with the prowess of Arjuna and the strength of Bhima, how will they overcome the strength of the incomparable three – Karna, Drona and Bhishma in battle? My hands tremble when I think of what grandsire Bhishma is capable of, having seen his unsurpassed abilities with my own eyes on many occasions. And how will

A Mother's Dilemma

Arjuna or Yudhisthira or Bhima upstage their illustrious teacher, Dronacharya who taught them everything that they know when it comes to weapons? Even now my legs shudder when I imagine the prowess of Drona."

As tears continued to flow down her cheeks, Kunti thought to herself, "Surely there is no way to kill these two grandmasters of weaponry who have been through countless wars in the past and carry with them decades of battle experience. And then there is Karna. Even if both Bhishma and Drona hesitate to kill my sons for sentimental reasons, surely Karna has no such qualms and is eager to win the war for his friend Duryodhana. He is an impressive fighter and will not hesitate to kill any of my sons if the opportunity presents itself."

Consumed by grief and fear for the safety of her sons, Kunti decided to take matters into her own hands. She concluded that it is now time to tell Karna the truth of his actual birth and family, and possibly salvaging the safety of her sons and perhaps even avoid the seemingly-inevitable war. In her mind, Kunti believed that if Karna defected to the side of the Pandavas, Duryodhana would eventually lose heart after losing his closest friend and ally, and war could be averted. But alas, how little did she understand her first born.

Carrying hopeful wishes of avoiding a destructive war, Kunti sought out Karna on the same banks of the river where King Shantanu met his wife Ganga all those years ago, knowing that Karna usually spends a part of his morning in prayers to the Sun God on these banks. Spotting Karna from a distance, Kunti walked slowly towards the warrior and waited tolerantly for Karna to finish his morning prayers. Karna was in deep meditation and was not aware of his surroundings until the sun started to burn brighter, and he slowly came back to consciousness before ending his morning prayers with a final salutation to the sun.

A Mother's Dilemma

As Karna finished his morning prayers and started a slow walk back to his chariot, the warrior noticed the queen mother, Kunti waiting patiently for him with under the burning sun. Amazed by this sight, he quickened his pace to a slow run and upon reaching the mother of the Pandavas, felt at her feet for her blessings, "Blessed is Karna, son of Adhiratha and Radha, to have the queen of the Kuru Dynasty waiting for him. Command me and your wish will be mine to deliver." Not obtaining a reply from Kunti, Karna was astounded to find the queen literally shaking with tears in her eyes, unable to speak.

Not knowing how to react, Karna tried again gently, "Dear queen mother, forgive me if any action of mine has unknowingly caused your any kind of distress. Karna is at your service, tell me what I can do for you. Any wish of yours will be granted as long as this soul is able to perform it."

Reassured by Karna's words, Kunti slowly gathered control of herself and held Karna up by the arms, addressing him such, "O Karna, you have no idea of how pleased am I to have finally be able to see and touch you with my very own hands. You are not Adhiratha or Radha's son my child, far from it. You are born of the fiery Sun God, Surya through a boon this foolish queen used in her teenage years, not knowing of the consequences that very action would have not only on you my poor son, but also on the rest of our family. Know that I am your mother, your very own, and never have I been happier than now, having my first born with me."

Karna Promises

Kunti's revelation stung Karna into a pang of helplessness as he struggled with the many emotions that he felt at that very moment – relief of finally knowing his birth parents, delighted with the knowledge that he was son of the mighty Surya, and anger towards Kunti for abandoning him when he was a baby, though at the same time he felt pity towards his mother and her plight during her teens.

To an extent, Karna also felt guilt and remorse for attempting to hurt his brothers in the past, and possibly in the future. Without realizing tears started to roll down Karna's eyes, wetting his upper garments as he stood like in a trance, his hands forced to hold his almost-bursting head while he struggled to absorb the revelations of the day.

While Karna was struggling emotionally, Kunti embraced her first born and between tears, continued, "Enough of this enmity against your brothers. Come back to us, forget what had happened in the past, and claim your rightful place within the kingdom. Naturally you are my firstborn and the rightful king. I know Yudhisthira, he will be more than happy to give up kingship once he knows that you are my firstborn, and together with your brothers you can rule the kingdom wisely. Just as you have transformed the kingdom of Anga under your rule, imagine what you can accomplish with your brothers under the guidance of wise teachers such as Vidura and Bhishma."

How little did she understand Karna. Not only is he fiercely loyal to those that stood by him, he is also an absolute advocator of dharma. Kunti's words brought him back to his senses, and he finally understood why Kunti sought him out just before the war.

To her words, Karna replied, "O mother, while your earlier words generated happy tears in my eyes, you have now shown me your true vile purpose of why you have made your way here today. If I was indeed as precious to you as you claim, why did you not proclaim this truth of my birth all those years ago when I was insulted in the assembly who refused to allow me to release my arrow simply because I was not a prince? Instead you let me suffer the ignominy of being laughed at by hundreds of inferior archers, something that only my friend Duryodhana saved me from."

In anger, Karna continued, "What kind of a person would leave his true friend the night before battle to join his enemies? I would be branded as not only a traitor but also a coward, and I have no intention of forsaking brave Duryodhana who was my only solace when I needed a friend most. To abandon him now would not only be a taint on my character, but would also be completely against the qualities I have always lived for. Now is not the time to leave Duryodhana and his brothers, not when they need me most in battle, especially not for someone who has forsaken me all these years but only now has sought me out to fulfil her own needs."

Even in anger, Karna's naturally generous disposition stood out, and he said to Kunti, "I am sorry mother, as I am unable to fulfil your wish. I will not leave Duryodhana now, not in his time of need. I will however promise you that I will cease from killing all of your other sons even after I defeat them in battle, with the exception of Arjuna. Hence you can go back in peace today knowing that either way you will still have five sons, but please do not harbour the hope of both Arjuna and myself surviving the war."

Kunti embraced Karna tightly, tears still flowing freely from her eyes. Karna looked at his mother's eyes that were filled with a mix of gratitude, amazement and sadness, and asked if there is anything else she wanted from him. In between tears, Kunti hardened herself and said, "My beloved son, none can challenge destiny, and that is the sole reason of why we are in this wretched situation today. As much as it hurts me, I understand and respect your decision and will not seek to change it anymore. I will live happy with the knowledge that none alive today is as steadfast to dharma as my first born, not even Yudhisthira, who is the son of Dharma himself."

"I have one final request; which I hope you will not say no to. Would you fulfil this wish Karna?" pleaded Kunti. Eager to be able to do something for his birth mother, a visibly-softened Karna replied, "I will mother. Command me and I shall obey."

Pleased with Karna's assurance, and instigated by Krishna's strange request some time ago when they last met,

Kunti proceeded to ask, "O Karna, I request that you do not use Indra's Shakti more than once on the battlefield, accept this as my last request from you."

Without flinching, Karna agreed before continuing, "I promise you mother, I will use only the Shakti once on the battlefield, and I shall not draw the weapon a second time. However, may I request that we keep what we have discussed today between us, and not disclose the truth of my birth to anyone else? Can you promise me this?"

In between tears and embraces, Kunti submitted to Karna's request, and after holding her son in her hug for the last time, took one final glance at her first-born and hurried back to Hastinapura. It should be noted here that Karna had earmarked the Shakti to be used on Arjuna, and was fully confident that one attempt with the deadly weapon would be sufficient to slay Partha.

Just a few days before Kunti sought out Karna, Indra will disguise himself as a wandering brahmana and approached Karna for a wish that Karna was more than happy to grant despite knowing that the request will weaken him considerably. Indra was aware that Karna would never refuse the wish of anyone that approaches him after his morning prayers, provided he can fulfil the wish. Karna was already forewarned the day before by his natural father Surya that Indra will seek to weaken Karna just before the start of the war, in fear of Karna killing his son Arjuna in battle.

Thus, when the sage mysteriously requested for his natural armour and earrings, Karna did not hesitate even a second and immediately cut them off his body and presented them, blood and all, to Indra. Indra, thoroughly amazed by

Karna's strength of character, regained his original lustrous form and graciously blessed Karna.

Overcome by guilt for trying to trick someone so noble, he asked Karna to ask for any boon that he wished for. Remembering his father's Surya's vision, Karna will reply, "O king of the gods, blessed am I to have seen you in your original form. If you must do something for me, please bless me with the knowledge of drawing and releasing your lethal Shakti weapon."

Indra will then award Karna with the Shakti; one that would eventually cause the Pandavas extreme grief on the battlefield. Indra will also heal Karna of all his wounds that he obtained during the removal of his natural armour. However, thanks to the promise that Kunti drew from Karna (at Krishna's behest), the warrior will be restricted to using the Shakti only once, and was not able to draw it again when it really mattered.

Krishna, who knew of Karna's divine birth, would also attempt to convince Karna to pledge allegiances to the Pandavas, but Surya's son would remain loyal to Duryodhana despite knowing that he will be fighting his own brothers. Having tried to convince Karna and failed, Krishna understood that nothing could sway the son of Surya from the path of duty, and blessed Karna with these words, "Karna, let your dharma always protect you from danger and evil, and may you attain the glories that you seek or die an honourable death trying!"

During the war itself, Karna will have opportunities to slay not only Yudhisthira but also Bhima and Sahadeva on separate occasions, but remembering his promise to Kunti, allowed her children to leave the battleground alive carrying nothing but superficial injuries and bruised egos. His eyes were set on the great Arjuna, and he did not swerve from that path or the promise that he made to his birth mother until the end.

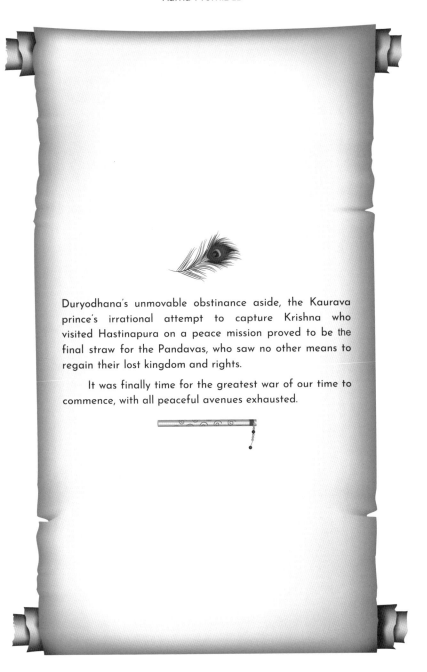

Duryodhana's unmovable obstinance aside, the Kaurava prince's irrational attempt to capture Krishna who visited Hastinapura on a peace mission proved to be the final straw for the Pandavas, who saw no other means to regain their lost kingdom and rights.

It was finally time for the greatest war of our time to commence, with all peaceful avenues exhausted.

Part Three

The War

THE GREAT WAR BEGINS

Preparations for the battle were well underway, and the groundworks concluded with the selection of a general commander of each army.

The Pandavas gathered all their troops and aligned themselves within seven separate battalions, with Bhima, Drupada, Virata, Satyaki, Sikhandin, Dhristadyumna and Chekitana appointed to lead the battalions. A meeting to choose the supreme commander was then held amongst the Pandavas, with Krishna in attendance. Krishna and Yudhisthira will seek the view of each Pandava one after another, starting from the youngest. Sahadeva will endorse Virata as his choice, while Nakula will endorse his father-in-law, the courageous Drupada as his selection.

When asked the question, Arjuna will propose that Dhristadyumna be made leader of the army, while Bhima will be of the opinion that there is none more suitable than Sikhandin, who is believed to be ordained to kill Bhishma in battle. After carefully taking into account all opinions, Yudhisthira will announce Dhristadyumna as the overall commander of the Pandava forces, with Krishna's endorsement of Arjuna's choice proving to be crucial in making the decision to appoint the destined slayer of Drona as their supreme general.

The selection of the general commander of the Kaurava forces was a much more straight-forward affair, with the Kauravas unanimously endorsing grandsire Bhishma to be the supreme leader of their eleven divisions. Recognized as the leader supremo of his clan for decades, Bhishma's strength at arms is unparalleled, he forced even the great Parasurama to submit to defeat in battle.

Bhishma will accept the leadership of the army, albeit with one condition – he will fight to the utmost of his abilities but will not kill the Pandavas who are his own grandsons. Duryodhana would reluctantly accept this condition as he knew that victory was almost certain with Bhishma at the helm.

It must be noted that Bhishma's constant belittlement of Karna's abilities will cause Karna to withdraw from the army a day before battle, causing great distress to Duryodhana. Karna will however be adamant not to take part in the war while Bhishma remains the commander of the army, and will stay off the battlefield until the tenth day of battle when the circumstances changed dramatically.

Just before battle commenced, Arjuna would famously experience an emotional meltdown, as he faced before him not just allies and friends but also his own family, now about to slaughter each other without mercy. The emotional collapse would then become a physical breakdown as his hands trembled and he dropped his bow, his body shivering at the sight of thousands waiting to kill each other.

At this juncture Krishna will intervene, console and proceed to educate his greatest devotee on the importance of upholding his dharma and carrying out the task at hand. Krishna's entire teachings, believed to be presented in poetry form to Arjuna, is generally believed to be the word of god, the essence of which is known today as the Bhagavad Gita.

The Bhagavad Gita teaches us amongst other things the importance of being devoted to duty and dharma, without worrying about rewards or attachments. Having heard Krishna's wisdom, an invigorated Arjuna will gather himself and armed with the Gandiva, prepare himself for battle.

As everything was ready for battle to commence, soldiers of both armies looked on in utter disbelief as Yudhisthira removed his armour, dropped his weapons and approached the Kaurava side. Wrongly assuming that the eldest Pandava was about to surrender having seen the size of the Kauravas forces, the Kaurava army started mocking him and eventually cheered, thinking that the war had been won without a fight.

Yudhisthira ignored them and continued directly towards Bhishma, whose feet Yudhisthira touched before saying, "Forgive us grandfather, as we have dared to challenge even you to battle today. Bless us with victory as we seek to uphold dharma and allow us to commence battle, unconquerable warrior."

Bhishma will have tears in his eyes as he blessed Dharmaputra, "Today I stand a joyful witness to the greatest of the Bharata race, one that is a worthy son of his father Pandu and the lineage that he follows. I am forced to serve the king of Hastinapura due to the oath that I took many years ago and will fight on the kingdom's behalf to the best of my abilities, but dharma is on your side and thus you will not experience defeat."

Having received Bhishma's blessings, Yudhisthira will proceed to obtain benedictions of both Kripacharya and uncle Salya, before lastly obtaining teacher Drona's blessings. Only once he was back in his chariot were the conches subsequently blown, marking the start of the war.

The first day's battle went the way of the Kauravas, with Bhishma causing havoc amongst the Pandava army and destroying thousands of troops and soldiers. Virata lost two of his sons on this day, Uttara who was killed by Salya, and Sveta who will be brought down by Bhishma's arrow shortly before the fighting ended for the day.

The second day of the battle could not have gone more differently than the first, with Arjuna keeping Bhishma at bay and Bhima wreaking mayhem amongst the Kaurava forces, completely annihilating the Kalinga forces and invoking fear in the hearts of the Kauravas with his lion roar wherever he went. When Bhishma's charioteer was killed, the uncontrolled horses bolted, carrying the chariot off the battlefield with Bhishma helpless; causing further panic in the Kaurava army that the Pandavas took complete advantage of. When dusk appeared, it was clear that the Pandavas had the better of day two, as they returned to their camps cheering.

The battle raged on for days, and just when the Pandavas felt that they were holding the upper hand, the combined might of Bhishma and Drona will bring them back to reality, equalizing the scale and bringing the Kauravas back into the fold. Thousands of soldiers fell each day on both sides, and as per rules of combat fighting ended at dusk each day before resuming the next day at dawn.

Back in Hastinapura, blind Dhritarastra would get detailed descriptions of the war at Kurukshetra from his assistant Sanjaya, who is blessed with divine eyesight and can choose to see as far as he wishes. Back on the battlefield, formations were countered by different strategies, with the Pandavas focussing on concentration rather than mass deployment as they have the smaller army. Bows were broken, swords crashed against each other, and mutilated bodies filled the battlefield, yet the war went on.

Bhima killed fourteen of Dhritarastra's sons on the fourth day and seventeen more on the eighth day, bringing unimaginable anguish to the old king. Many more of Dhritarastra's sons would have succumbed to Bhima's attack on the eighth day but for Drona's interception that allowed the princes to take flight to safety. Sikhandin will try to engage Bhishma many times, but true to his code of warfare of not wanting to fight a warrior who was born a woman, the grandsire will not engage Sikhandin and turned away each time.

Arjuna's son Iravan will cause great distress to the Kaurava army with his celestial Naga unit, until he was vanquished in a battle of illusionary mastery by the demon Alambusha. Seeing Iravan fall, Bhima's son Ghatotkacha would be enraged, and together with his rakshasa army and a frightening war-cry, fell upon the Kaurava forces like Death himself. Fighting together with his father Bhima, massive would the losses be for Duryodhana on that day as both father and son destroyed soldiers by the thousands.

The Great War Begins

Bhima will challenge and defeat Duryodhana, whose unconscious body survived only thanks to Kripa's timely arrival to rescue him while Jayadratha challenged Bhima to battle to sway the Pandava's attention away. Arjuna's son with Subhadra, Abhimanyu will wreak havoc and challenge even Bhishma and Drona, and make Kripa and Alambusha flee in defeat.

Thousands of warriors achieved the promised heavens for kshatriyas each day, while countless others remained on the battlefield, fighting each other simply due to the weakness of a monarch who could not control his foolish son.

Thus ended eight days of battle at Kurukshetra.

BHISHMA VANQUISHED

As the battle raged on day after day, Bhishma's prowess clearly exceeded that of everyone else's, even Arjuna's. Towards the ninth day's battle, Krishna will lose patience with Arjuna's half-hearted attempts at bringing Bhishma down, taking matters into his own hands. Dropping the reins of the chariot, he would jump to the ground, pick up a chariot wheel and approach Bhishma menacingly, wishing to bring an end to the grandsire's life.

Witnessing the sight of Krishna advancing towards him in fury, Bhishma will drop to his knees and accept his fate willingly, as dying at the hands of Krishna was undoubtedly the most noble of ends, earning automatic elevation to the heavens. To avoid having Krishna break his promise not to fight in the war, a distressed Arjuna would run after him. Partha will beg for Madhava's forgiveness and promised to make good his promise to kill the Kauravas and bring an end to the war. Only thus will Krishna be pacified by Arjuna's promise to fulfil his pledge. Battle then resumed until dusk called a halt to the ninth day's fighting.

The tenth day will be a significant one as it marked the last day of Bhishma's involvement on the battlefield. The morning started like any other, with conches and drums accompanying the weary bodies of soldiers back into battle, eager to win the war for their masters. The Pandavas altered their formation slightly, placing Sikhandin at the front of the army, as if signalling to Bhishma that his end was near. In response, Duryodhana placed all his generals around the grandsire, wanting to protect his commander at all costs. Bhishma himself seemed unperturbed by the happenings around him, as he knew destiny was all conquering and fate could not be altered.

With Sikhandin positioned in front of him, Arjuna took the fight to Bhishma, shooting arrows at the sensitive spots of the grandsire's armour from behind Sikhandin. When the arrows pierced his body, Bhishma felt anger rise within him, but checking himself, refrained from shooting his arrows at Sikhandin who completely blocked his view of his actual opponent, Arjuna. Greatly disadvantaged thus as Sikhandin's arrows unerringly struck its target without fail, Bhishma was not able to break Arjuna's bow or aim arrows at Partha, while Arjuna also continued to shower countless arrows on his grandfather.

Smiling now as he understood that this was destiny at work in order to bring him down, Bhishma found his bows broken one after another as arrows continued to shower upon his armour and more-damagingly, his body. Duhsasana will attempt to protect the grandsire, but will be put to flight by a determined Arjuna. Steeling his heart, Arjuna will then send two sharp shafts that would kill Bhishma's charioteer and smash his chariot into pieces, leaving Bhishma standing on the ground without his bow, or any cover. He would reach for his sword but Arjuna would shoot the weapon down even as Bhishma wielded it.

As the fatal arrows pierced his body for the last time, Bhishma would recognize them as Arjuna's arrows and not Sikhandin's, proving true to his dharma of not engaging a woman to battle even if it meant death. It is said that the gods themselves showered flowers and blessings on the old warrior from the heavens when Bhishma finally fell, arrows adorning the whole of his body as he fell headlong onto the grounds of Kurukshetra. His body will not touch the ground however, considering all the arrows that were sticking out of his shattered armour that provided a bed of arrows from which he finally admitted defeat.

As celestial drums were heard from the skies and a fragrant breeze took over the battlefield, both armies stopped fighting and encircled the fallen warrior. Duryodhana was inconsolable, his arrogance and confidence of winning the war suddenly absent. All the kings and princes stood around Bhishma with heads bowed, mourning the fall of the mighty grandsire, an unimaginable scenario until that very moment. Even Karna would rush to Bhishma's side when he heard the news, apologising profusely for all his faults in the past, yearning for the grandsire's blessings.

On his bed of arrows, Bhishma requested, "Could someone provide a support for my head please? It seems to be unsupported." Cushions from the camps were declined as Bhishma requested from his conqueror, "Could you release me from this discomfort as how a true kshatriya would, dear Arjuna?" Shaking with tears, Arjuna would then take out four arrows from his quiver, equip them with mantras and shoot them towards Bhishma.

The four arrows would attach themselves point up beneath Bhishma's head, providing him with the final headrest that he required. Smiling with satisfaction, he would thank Arjuna before requesting again, "My dear Partha, I am thirsty, could you get me some water to quench this tormenting thirst of mine?"

Understanding Bhishma's request and eager to fulfil it, Arjuna will once again reach for his arrow, charge it with an invocation and shoot the ground right next to Bhishma's face. And behold, a gush of water was seen escaping the ground at that very spot straight to Bhishma's lips, quenching the thirst of the old warrior. It was said that Ganga herself emerged from the grounds to release her son of his burning thirst.

Addressing all of those around him, Bhishma spoke, "Dear kings and princes, peace be upon you all. Take heed of the many deaths before me and my defeat today, and seek to cease fighting immediately. This alone is my desire as I lie here now facing north until my chosen time to leave this mortal body comes."

For the Kuru prince, Bhishma reserved these words, "My dear Duryodhana, did you witness how Arjuna quenched my thirst and provided me with my headrest? Is there anyone else alive today that is capable of such feats? May you be wise, cease from this foolishness and reconcile now with Arjuna and his brothers, else all will be lost and there will be nothing but utter destruction. Be blessed my child." Tragically even then, Bhishma's wise words would not sink in and Duryodhana would rush back to his camp, utterly displeased at the grandsire's admonishment.

Thus fell the unparalleled warrior Bhishma, the noble prince who undertook a terrible oath and surrendered his claim to the throne to please his father. Bhishma lived a faultless, full life, guided by dharma till the end, and inspired many long after his passing.

With Bhishma lying on his bed of arrows, awaiting his destined hour, Karna will join the battle and together with Duryodhana, installed Drona as the supreme commander of the Kaurava forces. In Bhishma's absence, the strategy shifted slightly with the new mission being to capture Yudhisthira alive, effectively ending the war once Dharmaputra becomes their prisoner. On the eleventh day of battle, Drona will launch a stinging attack on Yudhisthira, closing in after defeating Dhristadyumna and even breaking Dharmaputra's bow, only to be foiled by Arjuna's arrival to rescue his brother.

The next day, Arjuna will be forced to accept the challenge of Susharma's Trigartas who will undertake the terrible samsaptaka vow, and will be diverted away to another end of the battlefield, keeping him fully engaged. With Arjuna out of the way, Drona launched another attempt at capturing Yudhisthira, brushing aside challenges from renowned fighters such as Dhristadyumna, Drupada, Sikhandhin and Satyaki.

Only a joint challenge by all the remaining warriors and Bhima kept Drona at bay from taking Yudhisthira prisoner that day. Thus will Drona's multiple attempts to capture Yudhisthira be foiled by the various valiant warriors around him, much to Drona and Duryodhana's consternation.

Every war sees the emergence of young men fighting well beyond the abilities of normal men their age. Kurukshetra was no different, the land was blessed to witness many such young men surface, but none more outstanding than brave Abhimanyu and heroic Ghatotkacha.

VALIANT ABHIMANYU

One young warrior's name stands out from the rest whenever the great war is discussed; adolescent Abhimanyu, born of Arjuna and Krishna's sister Subhadra. Believed to be but 16 years of age when the war started, the young combatant had already gained great fame as a fearsome fighter, successfully living up to the legacy of his illustrious father. During the war, Abhimanyu will stand toe-to-toe with even Bhishma and Drona in battle, constantly lifting the mood of the Pandavas and causing grief to the Kauravas.

The thirteenth day will see Drona roll out the chakravyuha formation, knowing well enough that Arjuna and Krishna were engaged on another side of the battlefield with the samsaptakas. Only those two fully understood the science behind this formation, and were able to penetrate and break the chakravyuha formation. Abhimanyu did receive detailed knowledge from his father on how to pierce the formation, though critically he did not learn the science of exiting once within it.

In Krishna and Arjuna's absence, Yudhisthira will request Abhimanyu to penetrate Drona's formation, and the young warrior would gladly oblige, reminding Yudhisthira however that he can only breach the formation and not exit from it. Yudhisthira and Bhima would nevertheless urge the young Abhimanyu to proceed to break the formation, as they were confident that the Pandava army would be right behind him when the breach occurs to support him.

Heartened by the assurance of his uncles and the might of the generals around him, the fearless Abhimanyu would drive head-on into the formation, causing first a small break in the ranks of the Kauravas before slowly clearing enough space for an actual breach of the formation, allowing him to enter the chakravyuha right under the eyes of an astonished Drona.

But just as the rest of the Pandava warriors sought to take advantage of the breach and follow the gallant son of Arjuna, appeared the king of the Sindhu kingdom, Jayadratha to block their path. It must be noted here that Jayadratha had in the past received a boon from Lord Shiva to be able to check all the Pandavas except Arjuna once in battle, and he took full advantage of this boon to block the progress of the Pandavas with a supernatural display of courage, dexterity and determination. Bhima, Yudhisthira, Nakula, Sahadeva, Satyaki and the rest of the army tried their best but before their very eyes the breach closed and alas, Abhimanyu was on his own inside a foreign formation!

Unperturbed by the odds stacked against him, Abhimanyu upped the ante and slayed everyone in sight. It seemed to the Kauravas as if Yama himself had appeared on the battlefield in Abhimanyu's form, such was the destruction he caused. A fuming Duryodhana would challenge Abhimanyu but will be defeated in no time, with Drona having to rescue the Kuru prince from the wrathful young warrior.

Every fighter that dared to face Abhimanyu was put to flight; such was the devastation caused by the youngster. Fair play soon went out of the window, as a number of warriors attacked Abhimanyu simultaneously, seeing no other way to subdue the son of Arjuna.

The combined attack did nothing but raise the spirits of Abhimanyu, who resisted the onslaught while breaking the bow of each of the opposing warriors, one after another. Karna had his chariot smashed while Drona saw his bow broken time and again. Shakuni had to backtrack after having his armour pierced, while Duhsasana, Ashwatthama and Kripa retreated in defeat, unable to stand against the wrath of Abhimanyu. It was said that the gods themselves showered flowers and blessings on young Abhimanyu, as they witnessed the prowess of Arjuna's progeny.

Thus did Abhimanyu wreak disaster within the Kaurava ranks, rivalling even his father's abilities in battle. Sensing ultimate defeat unless Abhimanyu was checked, Drona will then instruct Karna to attack Abhimanyu from behind as five other warriors engaged Subhadra's son from all other sides.

Visibly struggling against his dharma, Karna will accept the instruction from his supreme commander and kill first Abhimanyu's charioteer and horses, before proceeding to break Abhimanyu's bow from the back. From the front and sides, Abhimanyu saw generals Kritavarma, Ashwatthama, Bhurisravas, Kripa and Drona himself approach.

Still the young warrior fought on undaunted, drawing his sword and shield and keeping all the great generals at bay singlehandedly. Karna was then forced to shoot down Abhimanyu's sword and shield, leaving Arjuna's son empty-handed, surrounded by opposing warriors. Without flinching Abhimanyu picked up a nearby chariot wheel, spinning it around and challenging all those around him.

But eventually the joint attack of the warriors overwhelmed a tiring Abhimanyu, whose chariot wheel was smashed to smithereens. Devoid of weapons, Duhsasana's son challenged Abhimanyu to a mortal combat, ending with the former killing Arjuna's son with a mace to his head.

Thus was courageous Abhimanyu finally killed mercilessly, with all fair conducts of warfare disregarded. Arjuna's grief knew no bounds when he learnt of his son's demise, but his fury reached tipping point when he heard of the manner of which the Kauravas killed Abhimanyu. Singling out Jayadratha to be the main cause of his son's death, Arjuna will then undertake an oath to kill the king of the Sindhu's before sunset the next day.

And successfully fulfil that oath he will, with Krishna creating an illusion of temporary darkness that will cause Jayadratha and the Kauravas to momentarily lose concentration as they falsely celebrated the arrival of sunset. A fatal mistake indeed, as a lurking Arjuna dispatched the deadly arrow with unerring accuracy, ending Jayadratha's life and avenging his son.

The fourteenth day of battle will see the demise of not only Jayadratha, but also Bhurisravas who will be slain by Satyaki, the latter having been on the brink of being beheaded until Arjuna shot down the sword-arm of Bhurisravas. Bhima will also kill thirty of Dhritarastra's sons on this day, causing both the old king and Duryodhana unspeakable anguish.

Towards the later part of the day however, Bhima will suffer a heart-wrenching setback of his own, the loss of his son from his asura wife Hidimbi; the young and valiant Ghatotkacha. These are the days of battle when fighting did not end at dusk but carried on into the night, an exceptionally advantageous situation for the asuras that see as well at night as they do during the day, hence are most damaging after the sun sets.

A TEST OF CHARACTER

Witnessing thousands of his men being slaughtered mercilessly by Ghatotkacha and his fearless asura army that night, Duryodhana became furious. Able to attack from the air, the asuras presented a fearsome sight, forcing Duryodhana to ask Karna to check the progress of their leader, the courageous Ghatotkacha who was doing all he can to impress his father Bhima.

With the Kaurava army losing numbers by the hundreds in the dark, unable to see their enemies, let alone defend themselves or counterattack, Karna considered his options carefully. He had Indra's Shakthi that would undoubtedly end the menace of Ghatotkacha once and for all, but he had already promised only to use the weapon once, and he was saving it for his inevitable battle with his sworn enemy, Arjuna. On the other hand, normal arrows and weapons were powerless against the asuras, and the army is losing numerous soldiers with each passing moment.

Karna's irritation at Ghatotkacha and his illusionary powers escalated to fury when one of Ghatotkacha's arrows hits him, injuring him on the shoulder. Instinctively, compelled by a sudden urge to kill the asura in the ongoing ruckus, Karna would launch the Shakthi on Ghatotkacha, killing him instantly and bringing down the young asura that wreaked mayhem within the Kaurava forces. Ghatotkacha's fall would produce completely contrasting moods within both opposition camps; while the Kauravas celebrated his death with loud cheers, the Pandava camp was besought by grief as they mourned the fall of the valiant young son of Bhima.

Karna would lament his action that led to the loss of the Shakthi, knowing that the chances of victory against Arjuna just diminished considerably. The fight continued into the night, and with Drona at the helm, the Kauravas rallied and attacked the Pandava forces gallantly. Only when Arjuna appealed to both armies to stop for the night did they finally pause, the common soldiers especially extremely grateful for the rest.

The fifteenth day of battle started with Drona on a killing rampage, destroying both the Panchala and Chedi armies mercilessly. He then turned his attention to the head of both forces, and in no time had severed the heads of both Drupada and Virata, much to the consternation of Dhristadyumna who witnessed the killing of his father first-hand. However, no one could check the progress of Drona who appeared to be possessed by a will to destroy everything within sight. Arjuna attempted to challenge Drona, but was unable to bring his preceptor to submission in a wonderful fight that it was said the gods themselves came to witness.

Watching the utter destruction wrought by Drona, a worried Yudhisthira shared his anxiety of facing possible defeat at the hands of the hands of their teacher. Hearing

A Test of Character

this, Krishna replied, "O Dharmaputra, it is true indeed that there is no way to defeat mighty Drona while he wields his weapons in fair battle. The only way he can be killed is when he is devoid of his weapons. And to achieve that, someone has to tell him that his son Ashwatthama has been slain. Only then will Drona lower his weapons, and then he can be eliminated."

Arjuna will be reduced to horror to hear Krishna's shocking suggestion, which clearly involved lying to kill an opponent. Bhima, who was also nearby, will however pounce into action and quickly get himself to the elephant corps of the Kauravas, where he knew existed an elephant with the same name of Ashwatthama. Without a moment's hesitance, he would bring his mace down on the head of the beast, killing it instantly. Knowing that Drona was fighting nearby, on the brink of releasing the feared Brahma-astra on the Pandava forces, Bhima then proceeded to shout in joy, "I have killed Ashwatthama! Ashwatthama is dead!"

Hearing Bhima's shouts, Drona's limbs became paralysed, his body physically responding to the shock before the brain was able to fully comprehend the situation before him. Eventually gathering himself, Drona will then doubt the truth in Bhima's words, remembering the boastful and pompous nature of the second son of Pandu. Seeing Yudhisthira standing in his chariot not far away, Drona shouted out to him, "Dharmaputra, you are well-known for your righteousness and live a life devoid of untruths. I hear Bhima claiming that he has killed my son Ashwatthama. I know of my son's prowess; he is not that easily vanquished. Tell me, is it true that my son is dead?"

Yudhisthira's body trembled, confronted by Drona's question. He knew admitting to the truth that the real Ashwatthama is very much alive and fighting on another side of the battlefield could be detrimental for the overall mission of the Pandavas, as Drona will continue to annihilate their army at will. The will to win reared its head strongly within him, urging him to accept the sin of lying for the greater good. On the other hand, the thought of uttering a lie for the first time in his life, in exchange for possible victory in battle, tortured his very soul.

Only Krishna knew what would happen next. He knew Dharmaputra too well. He knew that the son of Dharma would not lie, even if it meant victory in the war for the Pandavas. He knew that Yudhisthira will admit that it was Ashwatthama the elephant that was killed. But Krishna had a plan.

And he knew that he had to execute it perfectly. Or all would be lost.

Yudhisthira decided to win without deceit, or not win at all. He would not lie. He will admit to Drona that it was Ashwatthama the elephant that was killed, not the acharya's son.

Steeling himself to accept the consequences of his action, Dharmaputra will say, "Acharya, it is indeed true that Bhima had just killed Ashwatthama." Knowing that Yudhisthira was about to clarify that it was Ashwatthama the elephant, Krishna would at that pivotal moment pull out his conch and blow it as loudly as he could, completely drowning Dharmaputra's all-important next few words – "But not your son Ashwatthama, instead the elephant Ashwatthama."

A Test of Character

Thanks to Krishna's action and the pandemonium around the battlefield, the last few words uttered by Yudhisthira would never reach Drona's ears. And the damage was done.

Mistakenly comprehending from Yudhisthira that his son Ashwatthama was actually dead, Drona completely lost his desire to fight or live anymore, giving way to unimaginable grief. Oblivious to happenings around him, Drona will proceed to discard his weapons away before seating himself in his chariot in meditative state. Fixing his mind on the almighty Vishnu, Drona's attachment to all worldly matters disappeared, with Yudhisthira's subsequent shouts and pleas to clarify his statement falling on the deaf ears of his acharya.

Lurking nearby, Dhristadyumna would see his sworn enemy enter the state of yoga. Ignoring the calls of Yudhisthira and stunned warriors around him asking him to stop, the son of Drupada would then fulfil his prophecy of being Drona's slayer by decapitating the old warrior with one sweep of his sword, earning plenty of rebuke and condemnation in the process for his complete lack of chivalry in killing the old preceptor.

Thus was Drona killed, most agreed unfairly, by Drupada's son who emerged from the holy fire to bring an end to the mortal enemy of his father.

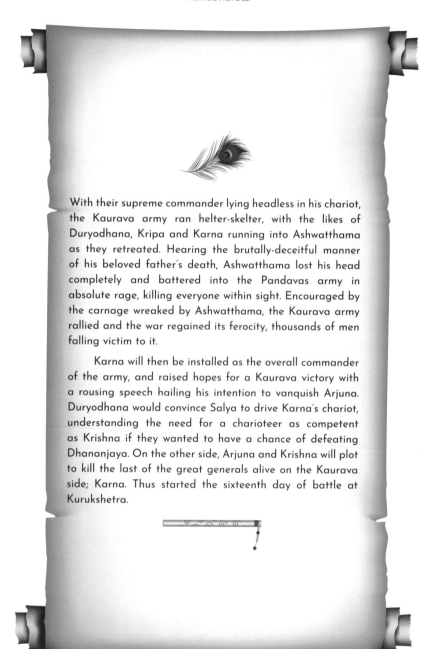

With their supreme commander lying headless in his chariot, the Kaurava army ran helter-skelter, with the likes of Duryodhana, Kripa and Karna running into Ashwatthama as they retreated. Hearing the brutally-deceitful manner of his beloved father's death, Ashwatthama lost his head completely and battered into the Pandavas army in absolute rage, killing everyone within sight. Encouraged by the carnage wreaked by Ashwatthama, the Kaurava army rallied and the war regained its ferocity, thousands of men falling victim to it.

Karna will then be installed as the overall commander of the army, and raised hopes for a Kaurava victory with a rousing speech hailing his intention to vanquish Arjuna. Duryodhana would convince Salya to drive Karna's chariot, understanding the need for a charioteer as competent as Krishna if they wanted to have a chance of defeating Dhananjaya. On the other side, Arjuna and Krishna will plot to kill the last of the great generals alive on the Kaurava side; Karna. Thus started the sixteenth day of battle at Kurukshetra.

THE DEATH OF KARNA

With Salya driving his chariot, Karna commanded the final remaining division of the Kaurava army. Ten divisions had been destroyed, but Karna remained defiant in upholding his kshatriya dharma and sought out Arjuna in his bid to win the war for his greatest friend, Duryodhana. Nakula tried to stop Karna from reaching Arjuna but was quickly subdued, the son of Madri not being in Karna's class. The son of Surya will send Nakula scampering to his elder brother Yudhisthira's chariot with his life intact however, remembering the promise he made to Kunti to not mortally harm any of her sons but Arjuna.

Yudhisthira will stand up to Karna's progress but will also quickly be made to surrender, and could not understand why the latter spared his life when he had the chance to kill him. Bhima would then try to challenge Karna but would have his attention swayed by the sons of Dhritarastra, sent to support Karna by Duryodhana. Licking his lips in anticipation of fulfilling his terrible vow of killing all of the blind king's sons, Bhima will decimate dozens of Dhritarastra's sons that day, with the surviving handful fleeing to escape certain death.

With Arjuna and Karna on a collision course, Bhima encountered a valiant Duhsasana, missioned with objective of protecting Karna at all costs. Remembering Duhsasana's unforgivable insult of Draupadi and the oath he took following that incident, Bhima would roar into battle, throwing everything he had at Duhsasana, bow and arrows first before physically destroying his opponent's chariot with his massive mace. Another swing would see the mace make contact with Duhsasana's forehead, bringing the evil brother of Duryodhana crashing to the ground, laying still with the body trembling as he saw death approach in the form of Bhima.

Bhima then dragged the limp body of Duhsasana around the battlefield, and with his sword will cut off the very arms that dragged Draupadi's hair. The son of Vaayu would then smash open the chest of Duhsasana with his mace, and the vile son of Dhritarastra would fortunately not be alive to see Bhima tear out his heart and drink his blood, just as he had promised to do during the insult of Draupadi.

The Kauravas shuddered in fear to see Bhima in such wrath, truly he did not appear human anymore with his face smeared with Duhsasana's blood. Even Karna was shaken by the sight and looked away, and did not see Bhima follow up the fulfilment of his gruesome oath by slaughtering another ten of Dhritarastra's sons.

Reminding Karna of his objective to slay Arjuna, Salya would direct the chariot away from Bhima and towards Arjuna. Arjuna encountered Karna's son before he reached Karna, and would ruefully have to kill the young warrior who fought valiantly, trying to protect his father. Karna's rage would boil over when he saw his son fall, and with a volley of arrows was upon Arjuna, who would in return send countless arrows of his own from the Gandiva.

The fight between Arjuna and Karna would be a truly magnificent spectacle, both being unparalleled bowmen and masters of celestial weapons, all of which were in full display as both warriors tried to subdue each other furiously. Arjuna's fiery Indra-astra was combated by Karna's smothering Bhargava-astra, while the former's celestial fire arrows were quickly equalized by the latter's extinguishing Varuna-astra.

Even Arjuna's Brahma-astra was successfully repelled by Karna, who in return directed the deadly Naga-astra onto his sworn enemy's neck. As the fatal arrow sped towards Arjuna, Krishna would press his foot down on the chariot, sinking the chariot into ground by a few inches and cause the weapon to hit Arjuna's war helmet instead of his neck. Karna's principles did not allow him to launch the same weapon again, thus a grateful Arjuna was saved from certain death by Krishna.

Seeing Krishna carry the chariot out of the ground before charging with Arjuna towards Karna, Salya then understood that the destined time had come. He would harass Karna by insulting the lack of prowess of Surya's son, while also speaking highly of Arjuna and Krishna's abilities in battle. Brushing off Salya's words as those of a bitter king that was forced to drive his chariot, Karna will attack Arjuna with renewed vigour as the son of Indra reciprocated determinedly.

Arjuna's relentless arrows broke Karna's bow, who was forced to lean against the side of his chariot for support.

Retrieving a new bow, Karna attempted to recall the mantras to the many celestial weapons that he knew, but was astonished to realize that he had forgotten the words of invocation. The curse of his teacher Parasurama would come to mind, and sadly would Karna realize that his end was indeed nearing.

When the wheels of his chariot got stuck in the mud, he found Salya refusing to help to lift the chariot and eventually abandoning Karna. Showering Arjuna with a flurry of arrows that temporarily blinded his opponent, Karna jumped to the ground and attempted to lift the chariot himself, only to discover that his renowned strength had deserted him.

And as the skies cleared, Arjuna found Krishna urging him to release the fatal arrows to end Karna's life once and for all. And reluctantly would Dhananjaya finally release three lethal arrows that would pierce disengaged Karna's armour, bringing an end to the life of the son of Surya.

Only after Karna's demise would the Pandavas learn of his actual birth, and understand why he had refrained from slaying them even when he had the opportunity, having promised their mother not to. Indescribable would be their anguish to learn that they had slain their noble eldest brother.

As Arjuna lamented on the sin of killing his own brother, Krishna will reprimand him and explain how Karna's fate and Arjuna's own success were already sealed by six different unbreakable reasons, mostly even before they stepped onto the battlefield, summarized for reading ease:

1. the curse of having his chariot coming unstuck in mud at his fated hour by a brahmana whose cow Karna accidentally killed.

2. the promise that mother Kunti obtained from Karna to use Indra's Shakthi weapon only once, not to be launched again.
3. the loss of his natural armour to Arjuna's father, Indra that reduced his strength considerably.
4. the curse of Parasurama that Karna would forget all the celestial weapons that he learnt when he needed them most, as Karna had deceived his teacher to be a brahmana, knowing Parasurama's hatred towards kshatriyas.
5. Salya's promise to his nephews, the Pandavas, that he would greatly harass and discourage Karna before his final battle with Arjuna to affect his state of mind.
6. Krishna's own protection of his greatest disciple, displayed in protecting Arjuna from the fatal Naga-astra that would have definitely killed Partha but for Krishna's intervention.

Thus did Krishna console an utterly-disconsolate Arjuna and convince him that he was merely a tool that completed the required task, one that was already pre-destined.

The disastrous news of Karna's death reached the Kaurava camp. Duryodhana was inconsolable. Kripa will attempt to pacify the Kuru prince and even proposed to end the war, but even in his lamentation Duryodhana's stubborn mind disregarded the advice of his teacher. Installing Salya as the commander of his remaining army, Duryodhana chose to fight until death. Salya will not remain the general for long however, as he will be killed by Yudhisthira's spear after a short but mighty battle.

Seeing the last of their commanders fall, the remaining soldiers of the Kaurava army lost all remaining optimism of emerging victorious. Sahadeva will personally attack Shakuni, and brought down the wicked uncle of Duryodhana with an arrow that will sever his head clean. Bhima will seek out all remaining sons of Dhritarastra and slay them all one after another, almost-fulfilling another of his terrible oaths- one that would be fully-accomplished only when Duryodhana himself is killed.

But where was the Kuru prince?

Seeing his entire army destroyed, leaderless and reduced to a handful of soldiers, Duryodhana felt anger rise within him like fire, burning his body immensely. Carrying his mace, he walked around, alone and aimless, attempting to douse the fire within him. A small lake, filled with clear, cool water caught his eye- and he made his way towards it with the hope that the water would cool down the scorching fire that burnt him from within. Entering the water, he settled down at the bottom of the lake, where he closed his eyes and reduced his breathing to almost non-existence, thanks to his yogic knowledge.

And in that state was exactly how the Pandavas found proud Duryodhana.

THE GREAT WAR ENDS

"I must admit that I am surprised to see you hiding in this lake, having caused the death of your tribe in entirety. Come out of the water like that warrior that you claim you are Duryodhana, and let's end this once and for all!" urged Yudhisthira. Hearing these words from his cousin, a stung Duryodhana replied, "Don't mistake my presence in this pool to be caused by fear. I am immersing myself in water to cool the fire that burns within me, not because I fear any of you."

Angered by what he assumed was Duryodhana's delaying tactics, Bhima bellowed, "Enough of this worthless talk. Do not attempt to camouflage the fear that you feel now with your petty excuses. It is time to end this war; step out of your hiding place or I will be forced to jump into the water and drag you out!"

To which Duryodhana replied, "Foolish Bhima, I have nothing more to fight for. I harbour no desire for the kingdom anymore. There you stand, all five of you while I am here alone. Dharmaputra, give me your word that you will all fight fairly in accordance to dharma when I emerge from this pond of water, and I shall step out now and defeat you all one after another!"

Yudhisthira half-sneered as he responded, "You dare to speak of fighting fairly when you attacked Abhimanyu with six of your strongest generals when the young boy was alone and unarmed. What dharma do you speak of, having discarded all of it at the assembly when you and your brothers insulted Draupadi. Nevertheless, you shall have your wish. We will not attack you in unison, instead we will give you the choice of choosing who you want to fight with, that too with the weapon of your choice. And if you defeat your chosen opponent, I will accept that you have won the war and you will be declared king!"

Krishna grimaced in disbelief when he heard these words of Dharmaputra. Here they were, on the brink of victory, and Yudhisthira was seemingly bent on giving the kingdom away, yet again! Krishna knew that Duryodhana was unparalleled in mace-fighting, having been tutored in the art by Balarama himself, even Bhima had only a slim chance of besting Duryodhana with the mace. And if Duryodhana chose to fight one of the others with the mace; surely they stood no chance against him and the whole war would end catastrophically for the Pandavas.

But Yudhisthira understood exactly how his cousin Duryodhana would react to his challenge. Dharmaputra knew that Duryodhana's pride would not allow him to choose a less-able opponent, though he was almost certain that Duryodhana would choose to fight with the mace. And true enough, the last remaining son of Dhritarastra chose that exact weapon, and to Krishna's relief, Bhima to duel with. The fight between the cousins raged long and hard, as both were supreme warriors with the mace.

Bhima's advantage of strength was easily equalized by Duryodhana's nimbleness and speed, and both fought without flinching despite being struck numerous times. As time went by Duryodhana's superior dexterity started to tell, as Bhima started receiving more blows without being able to return them, much to the distress of his brothers and Krishna. Understanding that Bhima's demise neared unless something drastic was done, Krishna loudly exclaimed to Arjuna that Bhima was yet to fulfil his oath of breaking Duryodhana's thighs, pointing to his own thighs as his eyes met Bhima's.

Bhima understood Krishna's cryptic message, and without any reservation brought his mace down on Duryodhana's right thigh, breaking it in one swift move. A shocked Duryodhana, who till then had the upper hand in the battle and did not expect an illegal blow under the waist, fell to the ground with a cry, lying there unable to move and defeated.

It was at that very moment when Bhima broke Duryodhana's thigh that Balarama arrived at the battleground, having returned from his pilgrimage of holy places, and the first sight to greet him was one of adharma. In anger Balarama raised his plough and advanced towards Bhima, who dropped to his knees and folded his hands in obeisance, succumbing to his fate to a visibly-furious Balarama. Krishna would run after this brother and pacify him, citing all the sufferings that the Pandavas had endured at the hands of Duryodhana as well as Bhima's own oath to redeem Draupadi's pride by breaking Duryodhana's thighs.

Thus was Balarama calmed, but not before he said, "O Bhima, for this act of treachery in attacking your rival below the navel, you will be known as one that practiced deceit to achieve your ambition. Duryodhana will on the other hand be celebrated as a righteous fighter till the end, and will automatically achieve the regions of eternal happiness!" Not wanting to spend even another moment there, Balarama jumped into his chariot and returned swiftly to Dwaraka.

The Pandavas retired to their camps, their joy of finally winning the war dampened by the manner of which victory was obtained, especially with the sight of proud Duryodhana lying mortally wounded on the ground occupying their minds. Ashwatthama would find Duryodhana on the brink of death, his anger rising as he heard of how Bhima ended his battle with Duryodhana.

Unable to control his fury, he will take a solemn oath to end the lives of the Pandavas, bringing much-needed joy to the grief-stricken heart of Duryodhana. On his deathbed, the son of Dhritarastra appointed Ashwatthama as the general of the Kaurava army, and instructed all remaining Kaurava warriors to henceforth follow Ashwatthama's guidance.

Discarding all kshatriya conducts and teachings of dharma, Ashwatthama would then lay a plan to kill everyone within the Pandava camp that night in their sleep. He shared his plan with Kripa and Kritavarma who were both astonished with the idea, and condemned Ashwatthama for even thinking of such a deplorable plan. Ashwatthama then highlighted how the likes of Bhishma, Karna, Duryodhana and even his father Drona were killed through strategy by the Pandavas, and in time had both Kripa and Kritavarma

The Great War Ends

on his side, willing to be his accomplice in carrying out his plan.

And on that moonless night after darkness had fully engulfed the land, the three of them approached the Pandavas' campsite fully armed. The remaining survivors within the camp were all fast asleep, having celebrated their victory earlier that day before retiring to their beds, dreaming of returning home to their families the next day.

But alas, dreams they will remain to be.

The trio of Ashwatthama, Kripa and Kritavarma will visit tent after tent, silently killing every remaining man, mostly in their sleep. Just like that, all the sons of Draupadi and the rest of the army were murdered in their sleep. The Pandavas themselves, Satyaki and Krishna were spared as they remained awake celebrating in their camp, unaware of the ongoing massacre of their army. Before leaving the campsite, Ashwatthama would set fire to the camps, ensuring that he killed almost the entire army that night.

Having successfully destroyed the Pandava army, Ashwatthama sought out Duryodhana, eager to inform the Kuru prince of his success before Duryodhana passes on. Hearing Ashwatthama's words, a tearful Duryodhana blessed the son of Drona, "O Ashwatthama, your words bring bliss to my ears! You have accomplished what neither Bhishma nor Karna could do! May you always remain blessed, as you have brought much joy to a dying soldier." With these words, Duryodhana took his last breath and expired.

Back at the Pandavas' camp, total pandemonium prevailed. Yudhisthira was completed broken by the turn of events, while a heartbroken Draupadi sought for someone to avenge the death of her children. All five of the Pandavas and Krishna pursued Ashwatthama, finally finding him hiding behind Vyasa by the Ganga.

Without any possibility of escaping, Ashwatthama will remove the jewel that formed part of his head and handed it to Yudhisthira, marking his surrender. Vyasa will forbid the Pandavas from killing Ashwatthama, exiling him instead to the forest, an act which effectively signalled the end of the destructive war.

The Great War Ends

Thus the great war came to an end, with the Pandavas emerging victorious.

Before heading back to Hastinapura, Yudhisthira and his brothers wanted to perform the last rites for their sons and the fallen warriors of the war. The bodies were carried to the bank of the Ganga, funeral ceremonies were flawlessly were performed and the bodies were then cremated on large pyres that were built along the bank of the river.

Having completed the rituals, the Pandavas followed Krishna as they made their journey back to Hastinapura. Their slow, hard journey home will be accompanied by lamentations of an utterly regretful Yudhisthira; for having to resort to a full-fledged war and causing the death of thousands in order to regain a lost kingdom.

Krishna would patiently respond to Dharmaputra, "O son of Pandu, do not give way to grief. You have done the right thing, and fought in accordance to your dharma and duty. A king must undergo hardships in order to restore natural order, and that is exactly what you have done. Do not lament, you have with you your brothers and Draupadi, and the time has come for you to finally take your place as the rightful king of this kingdom and rule it wisely, just as how your father and ancestors did before you."

Krishna's words provided some consolation, but Yudhisthira could not shake off the feeling of regret and melancholy as they reached the palace gates of Hastinapura, ahead of their meeting with Dhritarastra and Gandhari. Both the blind king and his queen were overcome by grief, having lost almost all of their children in the recently-concluded battle. They would however bless the Pandavas with prosperity and long lives, although Gandhari will be unable to hide her anger towards Krishna whom she believed could have changed the course of destiny, had he wished for it.

When Krishna presented himself before her, Gandhari will lose herself to anger, "O Krishna, for your impartiality towards the Pandavas and failing to be equal towards my sons, as well as allowing this great massacre to happen before your eyes even when you could have stopped it, receive my curse now. In exactly thirty-six years from now, you and the women of your clan will feel the exact same anguish that I feel now, devoid of my children. You will slay members of your own tribe with your own hands, and they will annihilate each other in brutal fashion as your clan will be destroyed. And you yourself will be killed shortly after without being able to protect yourself."

With the Pandavas looking on stunned by Gandhari's curse, Krishna replied, smiling widely, "O Gandhari, I accept your curse wholeheartedly. As you are well-aware, every beginning has an end, and I was worried of how the world would cope with the powerful Narayanas and Yadava warriors once I have left earth. For them to kill each other would be the only way for the world to be devoid of them. And for this I thank you, as you have removed a great burden off my shoulder. Now shake off your grief and welcome the sons of Pandu as how you would welcome your own, for they are sons of your husband's brother that are alike to your own."

Dhritarastra would then perform the funeral rites for his sons and followers before vacating the main golden throne, allowing Yudhisthira to claim the seat. Yudhisthira would however first return to the battlefield to obtain invaluable advice on kingship and general administration of the kingdom from Bhishma, who was still alive on his bed of arrows.

Once he had handed down all his knowledge to Dharmaputra, the old grandsire assumed a meditative state before permanently leaving his mortal body. The Pandavas held back their tears as they cremated their grandfather, with Yudhisthira lighting the pyre. Having scattered Bhishma's ashes in Ganga's waters, the Pandavas would then return to Hastinapura, marking the official start of Yudhisthira's reign as the monarch of the kingdom.

Krishna Chooses to Leave

The war had ended, and with it came the joys and agony that accompanied the conclusion of each war. Yudhisthira continued to rule the dynasty with his brothers in a fair and just manner, and was well-loved by his subjects while feared by enemies. Over the years Dhritarastra, Gandhari, Kunti and Vidura will retire to the Himalayas, leaving a huge hole in the hearts of the Pandavas and Draupadi. They were starting to discover that there was no such thing as true joy after a war of such gargantuan scale, despite them winning and regaining the kingdom.

Krishna had returned to Dwaraka after the war, and continued to rule for more than three decades. The tribe of Krishna, the Yadavas, spent their time dwelling in extravagance and over-indulgence, blessed by the wealth of the kingdom and devoid of external enemies to challenge their sovereignty. In time, Krishna realized that he was losing control of his luxuriously-indulging citizens who seemed to have also lost their humility and respect towards others.

It was such an instance when humility was found wanting that eventually caused the destruction of the entire

Yadava race, as foretold by Gandhari. When a group of learned rishis led by Narada made their way to Dwaraka to visit Krishna and Balarama, they were greeted by a group of drunk, arrogant Yadavas that not only forgot to welcome the rishis as decreed by the scriptures, but further humiliated the rishis by playing a joke on them. Disguising Krishna's insolent son Samba as a woman, they presented Samba to the rishis with a ball hidden under his clothes at the belly, and asked the rishis, "Tell us wise rishis, will this woman be blessed with a girl or a boy?".

The furious rishis saw through the whole joke and were beyond angry, and cursed the entire clan, "You Yadavas are drunk not only with wine but also in arrogance and insolence. You have dared to insult us such. This person will give birth not to a baby but to an iron club that will cause the end of your dynasty, with the exception of Balarama and Krishna!" Having uttered the curse in anger, the rishis then hastily left the city without meeting neither Krishna nor Balarama.

The visibly-drunk Yadavas laughed at the curse, though fear started to creep into them when Samba showed signs of labour and actually gave birth to an iron club a week later. Fearing the worst, Samba and the rest admitted what they had done to their king, Ugrasena, and sought forgiveness. Krishna was furious at Samba for his son's part in the mess, as he had proven time and again to be an extremely-insolent child that Krishna constantly struggled to manage.

Having consulted the wise men of the kingdom, the club was then ground into the finest powder they could produce which was then scattered into the sea off Dwaraka's coast. And in time everyone forgot about the curse of the

Krishna Chooses to Leave

rishis and fell back into the same stupor of over-indulgence, forgetting to worship their deities, ignoring the respect due to the sages of the kingdom, and even committed sins such as robbery and adultery without check.

The curse of the rishis was not far from fruition however, and constant dark omens were seen hovering over Dwaraka across the years, seemingly to remind the kingdom of its sins of the past. One day, the citizens of Dwaraka got together by the sea to celebrate a happy occasion, and drunk with free-flowing wine, started insulting and challenging each other. None realized that the spot they were celebrating on was the very same place where they got rid of the powdered iron club all those years ago. The powder had over time mixed with rain and sea water, and washed over the beach to magically form a dense bush of thorny reeds, growing quite magnificently over the beach stretch.

Amongst the Yadavas was Satyaki who fought on the side of the Pandavas during the war as well as Kritavarma, who fought on Duryodhana's side against the Pandavas. As the wine started to work its destructive magic, old quarrels started to reignite with Satyaki taunting Kritavarma on his actions of killing sleeping soldiers, while the latter responded by reminding the former of how he slayed weapon-less Bhurisravas who was immersed in yoga.

Soon the rest of the Yadavas joined the argument and the fight started to escalate to physical confrontations; culminating in Satyaki drawing his sword and chopping off the head of Kritavarma in one quick move. In response, the friends of the slain quickly took up arms and pounced on Satyaki, who struggled to defend himself. Wanting to defend the great general, Krishna's son Pradyumna entered the fight but both were eventually overwhelmed and found themselves mortally wounded.

Seeing his son killed by members of his own tribe, Krishna immediately sensed that the end was near. He understood that time was indeed ripe for the world to be cleansed of the powerful Yadava clan that had already reached its peak, and is now at its lowest ebb. Leaving the tribe on its own without his guidance as the world moved into the final age of Kali would expose the world to a great danger, something that he could ill-afford to do.

Willing the destruction of his very-own clan, Krishna looked around him for any form of weapon, and chanced upon the thorny reeds that have grown to almost as long as his arms. Without hesitation he plucked the reeds and started slashing everyone within reach. Magically the reeds altered themselves into the form of iron clubs, and within minutes everyone around him was seen slaughtering each other with clubs, the site quickly transforming into one filled with numerous mutilated Yadava bodies.

Cursed by the rishis and willed by Krishna himself, the tribe of the Yadavas quickly eliminated themselves in the most efficient of manners. As predicted by the rishis, only Balarama and Krishna survived the massive carnage and walked away from the site unscathed.

Having overseen the destruction of his race, and realizing that the prophesied time for him to leave this avatar had come, Krishna embarked on his final journey. Eager to find some shade from the unforgiving sun which scorched him relentlessly, he found a nice, shady spot within some bushes under a large tree. As he rested here, Krishna witnessed his elder brother Balarama going into samadhi and gently leaving his mortal body, transforming into his original Anantha Sesa form before bidding farewell to the world of men.

Krishna also saw Varuna and many other demigods appearing before Balarama and offering their worship as his elder brother gently left his body. This incident marked the conclusion of Balarama's time on earth, fulfilling the mission of Vishnu's avatar during the challenging tail-end of Dwapara Yuga.

An overbearing sense of agony overcame Krishna as he saw his brother leave mortality, as joyful memories of his childhood with his brother in Vrindavan came back to flood his mind. Brushing off the anguish, Krishna then reflected on the years that have passed, and having convinced himself on the successful completion of his objective, fell into a deep, comfortable sleep that he did not intend to wake up from.

A hunter looking for deer nearby saw the form of Krishna on the ground from a distance away, and accidentally assumed that it was an animal that was resting in the shade. Without a second thought the hunter strung his bow and shot an arrow directly at Krishna, piercing the great man on his foot, mortally wounding him.

Krishna felt the arrow pierce him through the foot all the way into his body. He opened his eyes and witnessed all the gods and demigods bent in obeisance before him, wanting to see Krishna in flesh for the last time in his vibrant mortal form. Blessing them with a final smile, Krishna uttered the immortal words, "It is time" before breathing his last.

Thus departed the great Krishna from the realm of ordinary mortals, having fulfilled his avatar's mission before returning home to Godhead.

Note: For the historically-keen, Krishna was believed to have left earth in the year of 3102 BC at Golokdham Theerth, within the modern-day holy city of Somnath. The footprints of Krishna can be found here, marking the very spot where the divine being left his mortal body to return to his own eternal abode.

Krishna Chooses to Leave

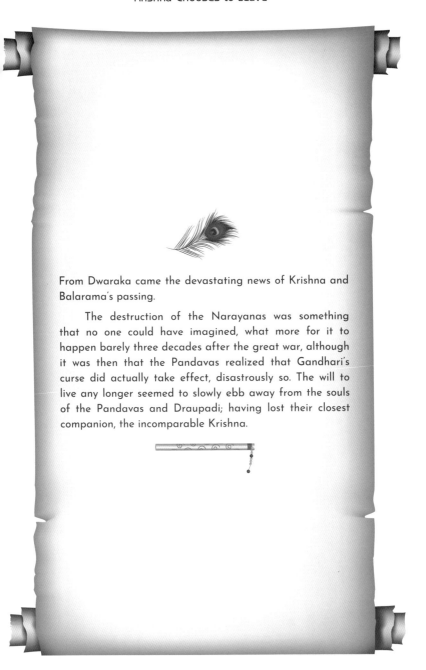

From Dwaraka came the devastating news of Krishna and Balarama's passing.

The destruction of the Narayanas was something that no one could have imagined, what more for it to happen barely three decades after the great war, although it was then that the Pandavas realized that Gandhari's curse did actually take effect, disastrously so. The will to live any longer seemed to slowly ebb away from the souls of the Pandavas and Draupadi; having lost their closest companion, the incomparable Krishna.

FOR THE LOVE OF A DOG

Thirty-six long years had passed since the Pandavas emerged victorious from Kurukshetra. It finally sunk in that they will not be seeing the ever-smiling face of their dear friend Krishna any more. In Yudhisthira's mind emerged the wise words of Bhagavan Vyasa who had previously highlighted the importance of following the natural path of seeking higher regions upon completion of worldly duties.

Yudhisthira consulted his brothers and shared his wish to depart, "The emergence of the age of Kali has never been as evident as now, dark omens are seen everywhere and sins are being committed by the people. Our dearest friend Krishna has also left us, leaving us orphaned as cows without a cowherd. I see no further purpose in our existence here, as we have exhausted all motives for our birth and being. It is time to seek higher abodes."

Having themselves lost all desire for life on earth anymore, his brothers and Draupadi readily agreed that it was indeed time to undertake their final journey, one that would hopefully take them to the heavenly realms. They were eager to be rid of their daily agonies that they carried with them every single day.

Yudhisthira consulted the elders and declared that Parikshit, son of Abhimanyu, will replace him as the monarch of the kingdom. As Parikshit was still young, Dhritarastra's only remaining son from the war, Yuyutsu, was declared as the regent until Parikshit came of governing age. Kripa was installed as the royal acharya to the kingdom, while the previous royal guru Dhaumya decided to return to his hermitage in the forest, where he would spend the rest of his life.

Donating all of their belongings to the brahmanas, the Pandavas and Draupadi gave up their royal attires and put on tree barks that suited the remaining days of their lives better. Looking like celibates, they bade goodbye to everyone at the palace and left Hastinapura, first completing a pilgrimage of holy places before reverting their path towards the Himalayas.

As they approached the highlands somewhere along the way a dog joined them, keeping them company and leading the way with Yudhisthira. None of them spoke to any other stranger along the journey, while also keeping their food intake to an absolute minimum.

Reaching the foot of the Himalayas, they came across a huge, blue lake by which stood the dazzling god of fire, Agni. Addressing Arjuna, Agni requested for the return of the famed bow Gandiva as well as the inexhaustible quivers which Agni presented to Partha many years ago.

More like an extension of a limb than a bow to him, Arjuna sorrowfully dropped the bow and the quivers into the lake, ceremoniously returning the weapons to Varuna, who was the original owner of the celestial bow and quivers. Leaving the lake, their journey now continued into one more gruelling, as the walk started to become an arduous climb. The Pandavas and Draupadi started to struggle with not only the climb but also effects of altitude, with physical limitations starting to show.

Draupadi became the first to fall, being the youngest and more delicate than the rest. Unable to take the physical exertions any more, her body succumbed and she fell to the ground, lifeless. The brothers witnessed her death, but without giving way to grief continued on their way. Next to fall was the youngest Pandava, Sahadeva, known to be the most knowledgeable of the brothers and a peerless chariot warrior in his prime. He gave up his life after climbing a particularly steep part of the mountain, the body unable to cope with the altitude or cold anymore.

A few moments after that Nakula followed his twin brother, falling to the ground lifeless, his body powerless to carry him any further in the unforgiving conditions of the mountains. Nakula was remembered as the best-looking Pandava, with a sharp intellect and an excellent swordsman.

As he lamented for Draupadi and his half-brothers, destiny dictated that Arjuna was to fall next, the once-famous warrior who dared to challenge even Lord Shiva to battle surrendering to the unyielding cold and his failing body. As Partha's body started to become blue, a visibly-grieving Bhima hurried to catch up with Yudhisthira, who had continued on, loyally accompanied by the dog.

Even mighty Bhima could not catch his elder brother however, as he felt the last of his renowned strength leaving his frame. In the end, Bhima found himself powerless to take even another step, and fell like a giant log onto the snow-filled ground. Yudhisthira turned back when he heard the last of his brothers fall, and after taking one last glance at Bhima's fallen figure, surged on to the summit.

His mind locked in meditative state, Yudhisthira and the dog continued on doggedly until they reached the peak of the mountain, where he saw a stunningly-bright chariot approach. Finding Mataali driving the chariot and the god of gods, Indra himself seated magnificently in its centre, Yudhisthira bowed his head and folded his hands in respectful prayers.

Greeting Dharmaputra cheerfully, Indra invited the Pandava into the chariot, promising to take him to the heavens. To which Yudhisthira replied, "O Indra, I desire nothing but to be reunited with my brothers and Draupadi who have all fallen victim to this mountain." Referring to the dog, Dharmaputra continued, "For now I am happy to look after this faithful companion of mine which had decided to accompany me throughout my journey and taken shelter of me."

A smiling Indra replied, "Respected Dharmaputra, your brothers and Draupadi have already discarded their physical bodies, and have ascended to heaven before you. Come with me and join them there. But pray leave the dog behind, as heaven is not a place for dogs." Refusing to board the chariot unless the dog too was allowed to come with him, Yudhisthira persevered, "Forgive me great god, I have devoted my life to saving the weak and helping those that have sought my shelter. If the dog does not come, nor will I."

What happened next defied ordinary logic. Before Yudhisthira's own eyes, the dog suddenly altered its shape, growing larger and larger until the god of justice Dharma himself stood in front of his son, smiling broadly. Embracing his son warmly, Dharma admitted that it was him who accompanied his son all along in the form of the canine, wanting to experience first-hand Yudhisthira's renowned adherence to dharma.

Dharma then addressed his son, "My child, today you have given your father the joy of knowing that there is no one alive, not even in the heavens, who match up to you in virtue or adherence to dharma. Go now with Indra to the godly-realms, where you will find not just your loved ones but heavenly bliss awaiting you. Go with my blessings my son."

Folding his hands in obeisance, Dharmaputra received his father's blessings and finally ascended Indra's chariot.

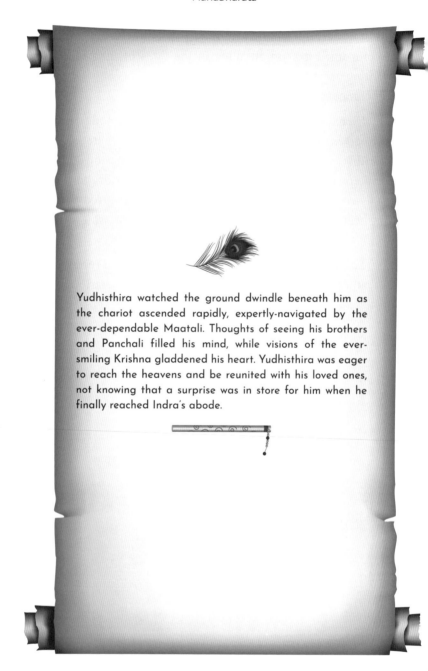

Yudhisthira watched the ground dwindle beneath him as the chariot ascended rapidly, expertly-navigated by the ever-dependable Maatali. Thoughts of seeing his brothers and Panchali filled his mind, while visions of the ever-smiling Krishna gladdened his heart. Yudhisthira was eager to reach the heavens and be reunited with his loved ones, not knowing that a surprise was in store for him when he finally reached Indra's abode.

EVERY BEGINNING HAS AN END

Yudhisthira reached heaven in no time, and the first sight that greeted him was one of the Kaurava prince, Duryodhana seated on a huge throne enjoying the benefits of Swarga. A surprised Yudhisthira looked around for his brothers but could not find them. Unable to hide his irritation, Yudhisthira questioned the occupants of the heavens, "Why is this envious and spiteful man seated in all glory here while my sinless brothers are nowhere to be seen? My only wish is to be reunited with them and Panchali, please take me to where they are immediately!"

Both Indra and Narada heard Yudhisthira's words, and the celestial sage was the first to respond, "Son of Dharma, words such as those do not belong here in heaven. There is no hatred in heaven, nor is there harbouring of ill feeling towards one another. Your cousin Duryodhana achieved his place in the heaven of warriors through his kshatriya dharma, which he upheld until the end of his life." Indra added, "Narada is correct Yudhisthira. Cast aside those ill feelings and enjoy the benefits of Swarga. You still hold such negative thoughts only because you uniquely arrived in heaven in your mortal body, which you should have already discarded."

To which Dharmaputra responded, "It is no wish of mine to remain with this sinner who was the single most significant cause of all our worldly sufferings. I want to be with my brothers and Panchali. I also do not see Karna here, one who was comparable in battle to Arjuna himself. When I think of how Karna resisted from killing me when he had the chance to, my eyes fill with tears knowing the battles that must have raged within him; whether to uphold his promise to Duryodhana or to keep his brother alive as promised to Mother Kunti. I must meet him and fall at his feet. Take me to him and my brothers now, I do not wish to remain here any longer!"

Hearing these words, Indra will instruct one of his assistants to take Yudhisthira to where he wanted to go. As Dharmaputra followed his guide, he realized that the atmosphere had begun to decay, with a horrible stench filling the air and dead bodies lying all along the path. The smell of dried blood and slime engulfed the air he was breathing in, while darkness filled the atmosphere, with countless evil spirits seen moving around. Bracing himself with a vision of finding light at the end of the tunnel, Dharmaputra was suddenly astounded to hear familiar voices calling out to him.

One voice said, "Stay a while o sinless one, your arrival has brought a fragrance so fresh that allows us to temporarily forget our suffering." Another lamented, "Do not leave us and go wise one, the sight of you allows us a bit of brightness in this horrid place. Stay with us!" Utterly confused, and still unable to place those voices, Yudhisthira asked, "Who are you, lamenting thus in anguish and wretchedness? Why do you suffer in this hell?"

To his bewilderment, the voices answered in a sequence that left him utterly shaken, "It is me, your brother Bhima." "It is none other than your eldest brother, Karna." "It is I, blameless Panchali my lord". "I am Nakula, brother". Yudhithira also heard voices of Arjuna, Sahadeva, Sikhandin and the rest of his loved ones responding to his question.

Overcome with grief but seething with anger, the righteous Dharmaputra would then proceed to condemn the very dharma that he had followed all his life without fail, and denounced the gods for the fate that had been meted out on the trapped souls. Sending the attendant back to Indra, Yudhisthira would then adamantly stay with his loved ones, denying himself the joys of heaven to be with those that had been faithful to him throughout their lives.

Thus passed a muhurtha, and before Yudhisthira's very own eyes materialized the gods Indra and Yama, surrounded by Narada and the other heavenly beings. With their arrival, the darkness and foul stench immediately disappeared, replaced with brightness and a fresh, fragrant breeze. Yudhisthira fell to his knees, hands folded in obeisance as he discovered that the lamenting voices had magically disappeared.

Dharmaputra found both Indra and Dharma beaming down at him, with his father speaking first, "Glorious son of mine, despite the many times I have tested you, you chose to be steadfast to dharma and even chose to remain in hell for your loved ones. It is indeed the law of order that even the best of men will need to experience hell, albeit for a little while. That was what you experienced a while ago, compounded by the illusion of having your brothers and loved ones in hell. None of them are actually suffering in hell, instead they are all happily living in heaven."

Indra then added, "Son of Dharma, discard your human body now, and deservedly take your place in Swarga with them. Without doubt, no mortal deserves a place in heaven more than you do. But look, you seem no longer human already!"

Dharmaputra then witnessed his mortal frame magically disappearing from sight as he slowly transformed into a god. All humanly emotions such as rage and hatred vanished with the disappearance of his body. The environment around him also changed into a portion of heaven where he saw not only his brothers and Draupadi but also Bhishma, Drona and the Kauravas; all having achieved Swarga and the state of gods. Surrounded by Indra, Dharma, Narada and celestial attendants, all of them looked radiant and joyful, having achieved a state free of all negative traits.

As he became immersed in the sight of all of them enjoying transcendental happiness, Yudhisthira discovered that he had finally achieved what he had always desired; serenity, peace and true contentment.

Epilogue

The timeless epic called the Mahabharata has captivated millions of us, me definitely being one of them. Having been intrigued by the stories of this great epic for years, I have over the last few years taken time to visit some of the more significant sites mentioned in the epic. For the historically-inclined, my revelations would hopefully encourage you to visit some, if not all of the sites yourself, and probably you would then be able to relive the epic in your own personal way.

Let us start with Kurukshetra, where the great war was believed to have occurred. Located about a 3 hour-drive away from Delhi, the ancient war site of Kurukshetra is today a sprawling city, no different to any other Indian city. Close to Kurukshetra one would find Jyotisar, the site believed to be where Krishna delivered the Bhagavad Gita to his closest disciple, Arjuna just before the start of the great war. The exact spot would be beneath an ancient banyan tree, one that is revered even today and receives hundreds of visitors each day.

Close to the main city of Kurukshetra, one would find the town of Thaneswar, where the ancient Sthaneshwar

Epilogue

Mahadeva temple is located. This revered temple was believed to have been visited by Krishna and the Pandavas just before the beginning of the war, as they were eager to receive the blessings of the great god Mahadeva before commencing battle.

One would also find the impressive Sri Krishna Museum in Kurukshetra, where you would find arguably the best visual representation of the Mahabharata anywhere in the world, presented to you via larger than life visual art exhibitions. Close by you would also find Bhishma Kund, believed to be the very spot where Bhishma rested on his bed of arrows, thirsty and seeking water. And that is when Arjuna will shoot his arrow into the ground and water would sprout out from this exact spot, quenching Bhishma's thirst.

Moving on to Somnath, here one would find the exact spots where Krishna was shot by the hunter Jara as well as the spot where he leaves his mortal body and returns home. The former would be Bhalka Tirth, while the latter can be found at Golokdham Tirth. Both locations are a few minutes away from the Somnath Jothirlinga temple, and are popular tourist destinations today.

Blessed I am by Krishna to have visited all of the four Char Dham of Hinduism, and I arranged my journey such so that my last location would be Krishna's very own kingdom, Dwaraka. Although Dwaraka seems to be a shadow of its former past, the Dwaraka that we see today is the modern city of Dwaraka, not ancient Dwaraka. Existent as part of present-day Gujarat, it remains an absolutely beautiful city built along the same sea straits where ancient Dwaraka used to be, with dusk being my favourite time of the day here as

Epilogue

you get to watch the sun setting gorgeously every evening by the sea.

It was believed that Krishna forecasted that the seas would swallow his kingdom exactly seven days after he leaves earth, and the scriptures record that this is exactly what happened upon Krishna leaving his mortal body, with heavy storms and huge waves engulfing Dwaraka until there was no trace of the kingdom any more. In modern Dwaraka, one must visit the outstanding Dwarkadheesh Temple, as well as pay a visit to the ancient island of Beyt Dwaraka, believed to be a favourite resting place of Krishna.

I have also been lucky enough to visit both Mathura, where Krishna was born and Vrindavan, where young Krishna grew up with father Nanda Maharaja and tended to cows with brother Balarama. In Mathura one would find Krishna's birth temple, better known as Shri Krishna Janmasthan Temple. Mathura is also well-known as the spot where Krishna killed his evil uncle Kamsa and rescued his grandfather Ugrasena who was imprisoned by Kamsa.

My journey also took me to modern day Varanasi (Kasi), where Bhishma had won the princesses Amba, Ambika and Ambalika at the swayamvara conducted by the King of Kasi. A visit to Varanasi would expose you to the unique experience of a truly-ancient city that continues to thrive in the modern era. Truly have I not come across such an aura or experience of ancient traditions being upheld within an entire city anywhere else in the world. Kasi is as ancient as it gets, even today.

May you find as much joy and satisfaction in discovering the above places (and others that I may have missed) as I did. Truly life itself is the greatest eternal journey of discovery.

I bring an end to this book with one of my favourite quotes from the Bhagavad Gita, words of Krishna himself:

> *Whenever virtue declines and unrighteousness dominate; I incarnate as an avatar, in visible form I appear from age to age to protect the virtuous and to destroy the wicked and evil in order to re-establish righteousness.*
>
> *Bhagavad Gita 4:7–8*

GLOSSARY

Abhimanyu	Son of Arjuna and Subhadra, he also married King Virata's daughter Uttara and provided the continuation of lineage for the Pandavas through his grandson Parikshit.
Adhiratha	father of Karna, he was the leader of the charioteer clan called the sutas. He found Karna as a baby, floating in a basket along the river after his actual mother Kunti had discarded him.
Agni	the god of fire. He is usually invoked before any sacrifice to purify the offerings.
Alambusha	demon ally of Duryodhana who fought on the side of the Kauravas, slayer of Arjuna's son Iravan. He bore an enmity towards Bhima who had killed his brother Baka.
Amaravathi	Indra's heavenly realm

Glossary

Amba	eldest daughter of the king of Kasi, who will be reborn as the daughter of Drupada but will reincarnate and transform into a male called Sikhandin to exact revenge over Bhishma.
Ambalika	sister of Amba and Ambika, and mother of Pandu.
Ambika	sister of Amba and Ambalika, mother of Dhritarastra.
Anantha Sesa	the endless form of Vishnu in naga form, and believed to be the original form of Balarama. His omnipresent protective nature is displayed in how Balarama protects his younger brother Krishna.
Anga	the kingdom that Karna ruled, thanks for Duryodhana's generous gift when he was insulted in the assembly of warriors.
Antardhana	Kubera's celestial weapon, the mace.
Arjuna	the third Pandava, fathered by Indra through Kunti's divine boon. Famously-known as the greatest archer in existence. Believed to be an incarnation of Nara, Narayana's eternal ally.
Astra	a celestial weapon, usually infused with a powerful divine mantra.
Ashwatthama	son of Drona, grandson of Bharadwaj, master of illusionary warfare who killed all the sons of Draupadi and finally surrendered to the Pandavas, marking the end of the war.

Ayodhya	the kingdom of Shri Rama, the seventh incarnation of Vishnu.
Bakasura	a man-eating demon that was killed by Bhima in Ekachakra village.
Baladeva	another name for Balarama (see Balarama).
Balarama	elder brother of Krishna, an incarnation of Vishnu. Did not take part in the war of Kurukshetra as he did not want to be impartial to either side.
Bhima	the second son of Pandu, fathered by Vaayu through Kunti's divine boon. Known to be the strongest of the Pandavas in might though with a fiery temper, he was also the half-brother of Hanuman.
Bhishma	the eighth son of Shantanu, mothered by Ganga. The grandsire of the Kuru kingdom, he was formerly known as Devavrata. He looked after the Pandavas when they returned to Hastinapura with Kunti upon the death of Pandu. The first commander of the Kaurava army tried in vain many times to prevent war from breaking out but failed. His teachings on virtue, duty and religion to Yudhisthira while he was on his bed of arrows formed the Shanti Parva in the original text of the Mahabharata.

Bhurisravas	grandson of Balhika, who was brother of Shantanu. He fought on the Kaurava's side at Kurukshetra, and died at the hands of Satyaki after having his sword arm cut off by Arjuna.
Brahma-astra	an unstoppable divine weapon that originated from the creator, Brahma himself. Believed to be the most destructive of astras.
Chakravyuha	a complicated battle formation in a disc/lotus shape that was used by Drona to combat the Pandavas.
Chekitana	a fearsome warrior, he led a division of the Pandava army at Kurukshetra.
Chitrangada	first son of Shantanu and Satyavati who became the monarch of Hastinapura after his father. He was killed by a gandharva king.
Daruka	the esteemed charioteer of Bhagavan Sri Krishna.
Devavrata	another name of Bhishma before he took his terrible oath of celibacy. In his previous life Devavrata would be a celestial Vasu who received the curse of Vasistha to be born on earth for the sin of stealing the sage's ceremonial cow.
Devendra	another name of Indra, king of the demi-gods and father of Arjuna.
Dharma	another name of Yama, the god of dharma and righteousness. He was also

	the father of Yudhisthira, who thus was also known as Dharmaputra (son of Dharma).
Dhananjaya	another name of Arjuna which means one that wins wealth.
Dharmaputra	another name of Yudhisthira, meaning the son of Dharma.
Dhaumya	the family priest of the Pandavas, who also accompanied them during their exile years in the forest.
Dhristadyumna	son of Drupada and brother of Draupadi, he was born from a divine fire to bring an end to Drona's life thanks to Drupada's penances. He was also the supreme general of the Pandava army at Kurukshetra.
Dhritarastra	first son of Vichitravirya and Ambika, father of Duryodhana and the Kauravas. He was born blind and was side-lined as king due to this.
Draupadi	daughter of Drupada, the consort of the Pandavas. She was born from the same divine fire that presented Drupada with Dhristadyumna, and is also known as Panchali.
Drona	son of Bharadwaj, the martial preceptor of the Pandavas and Kauravas. Father of Ashwatthama, he learnt martial arts from Parasurama and was an unparalleled warrior.

Drupada	father of Dhristadyumna and Draupadi, and king of the Panchala kingdom. Strong ally of the Pandavas.
Duhsasana	brother of Duryodhana, he insulted Draupadi by dragging her into the assembly hall by her hair.
Duryodhana	eldest son of Dhritarastra, and crown prince of the Kuru kingdom. He was killed by Bhima due to a blow to his thigh, considered illegal in mace fighting conduct.
Durvasa	a sage that is famous for his legendary short temper, though also generous with boons. Having tended to the sage's needs with utmost care when he visited Kuntibhoja's residences, Kunti will be awarded with the Atharvaveda mantra which would beget her children in the future, as the sage could foresee the difficulties her future husband would have to produce progeny.
Dushala	Duryodhana's sister, the only daughter of Dhritarastra and Gandhari. She had 100 brothers.
Dwaraka	the kingdom of Krishna and the Yadavas.
Ekalavya	a Nishada tribe leader who would be rejected as a student by Drona due to him not being of princely stature, but would turn out to be an archer of

	unrivalled skill until Drona asked for his thumb as homage.
Gandhari	wife of Dhritarastra and princess of Gandhara, she will blindfold herself for life after marrying naturally-blind Dhritarastra to share the same life experiences as her husband. Believed to have ascetic powers due to her constant penances and sacrifices.
Ganga	the sacred river goddess, also wife of Shantanu and mother of Devavrata.
Ghatotkacha	valiant son of Bhima and his rakshasa wife, Hidimbi. He was a master of illusionary warfare.
Gandiva	sacred bow of Arjuna, lent to him by Varuna.
Ganesha	Lord Shiva and Parvati's first son, believed to be the scribe of the original Mahabharata that was dictated without pause by Bhagavan Vyasa. Also known as Ganapathi and Vigneshwara.
Govinda	another name of Krishna, it means cow-herd.
Hanuman	valiant Vaanara (monkey) warrior who was Rama's greatest devotee, he was also Bhima's half-brother as they shared the same father, Vaayu.
Hastinapura	the capital of the Kuru dynasty.
Hidimbi	mother of Ghatotkacha, and asura wife of Bhima.

Indra	the king of the demi-gods, he is the father of Arjuna. Also known as Devendra.
Indra-astra	Indra's divine weapon.
Indrakeeladri	a mountain that Arjuna would climb before his encounter with Shiva.
Indraprastha	the new capital that Pandavas built and developed after leaving Hastinapura. Previously known as Khandavaprastha.
Iravan	Arjuna's valorous son from his Naga wife, Ulupi. He was killed by the demon Alambusha.
Janardhana	another name of Krishna, which means one that is worshipped and protects those around him.
Jarasandha	the famous king of Magadha, who was the reason of why Krishna relocated his kingdom to Dwaraka. Jarasandha was killed by Bhima in a wrestling contest before Yudhisthira could assume the title of emperor.
Jayadratha	the Sindhu king who closed the breach within the chakravyuha formation before the Pandavas could follow Abhimanyu into the formation, thanks to a boon from Shiva. He was killed by Arjuna the next day who identified Jayadratha as the cause of Abhimanyu's demise.
Kamsa	evil uncle of Krishna who jailed his own father Ugrasena, he was killed by Krishna.

Glossary

Karna	son of the sun-god Surya and Kunti, who was abandoned as a baby by his mother. He grew up with charioteer Adhiratha and Radha, and was a student of Parasurama. A peerless archer and valiant warrior, he was the third general of the Kaurava army before being killed by Arjuna under the guidance of Krishna.
Karthikeya	second son of Lord Shiva and Parvathi, he is also known as the god of war.
Kaunteya	the sons of Kunti, namely Yudhisthira, Bhima, Arjuna and also Karna.
Kaurava	the descendants of King Kuru.
Khandavaprastha	the ancient capital of the Kuru dynasty, it was renamed as Indraprastha after the Pandavas rebuilt it. Previous emperors such as Yayati and Nahusha utilized this city as their capital.
Kripa	preceptor of the Kurus, brother-in-law of Drona. He was also the chief priest of the Kuru dynasty, and is believed to be an avatar of Brahma.
Krishna	the eighth avatar of Vishnu, he was the son of Vasudeva and Devaki but grew up with Nanda Maharaja and Yasoda. Believed by many to be the master strategist that reigned on earth to get rid of all demonic kings, culminating in the Mahabharata war. Krishna will

	oversee the destruction of his own race, the Yadavas, before choosing to leave his avatar, an event that marked the start of Kali Yuga, the final age.
Krishnaa	another name of Draupadi.
Kritavarma	a fearless Yadava general who fought on behalf of the Kauravas in the war. Will be one of Ashwatthama's accomplices when they mercilessly slaughter the Pandava soldiers in their sleep.
Kubera	the celestial treasurer of the gods, some also call him the god of wealth. Also a Lokapala, he will bless Arjuna with his celestial mace after the Pandavas wins the grace of Lord Shiva.
Kunti	mother of the Pandavas and wife of Pandu, she is also mother of Karna who was born before her wedlock with Pandu. Also known as Pritha.
Kuntibhoja	adopted father of Kunti, who looked after Kunti when she was little as he was childless.
Kuru	ancient king who founded the Kuru dynasty.
Kurukshetra	the site of the great Mahabharata war that occurred for 18 days.
Lokapalas	the guardians of the four directions, namely Kubera (north), Dharma/ Yama (south), Indra (east) and Varuna (west).

Glossary

Mahadeva	another name of Shiva, which means the great god.
Mataali	the charioteer of Indra.
Mathura	Krishna's birth kingdom, where he also killed evil Kamsa.
Muhurtha	a unit of measurement used to calculate time, in modern calculation a muhurtha is considered similar to forty-eight minutes.
Muruga	another name of Karthikeya.
Nahusha	an ancestor of the Kuru dynasty.
Nakula	first son of Madri, the fourth Pandava was also the son of the Ashwini star.
Nara	divine pair of Narayana, in human form. Believed to be Arjuna during the time of the Mahabharata.
Narada	the celestial sage of the universe, one with unlimited ascetic powers. He was also known as Devarishi (the godly sage).
Narayana	Another name of Vishnu.
Narayana-astra	the celebrated celestial weapon of Narayana, amongst the most-deadly of astras.
Narayanas	the tribe of Narayana or Krishna.
Nagapasha	Varuna's celestial weapon, the noose.
Nishada	hunters or fishermen of aboriginal origins, usually treated as outcastes due

	to their birth. Ekalavya was an example of a nishada.
Panchali	another name of Draupadi, as she was the princess of the Panchala kingdom.
Pandavas	the five sons of King Pandu, namely Yudhisthira, Bhima, Arjuna, Nakula and Sahadeva.
Pandu	the father of the Pandavas, the second son of Vichitravirya and Ambalika who became the king of Hastinapura as his elder brother Dhritarastra was born blind. He died in the forest, caused by a curse from a sage.
Parasara	father of Bhagavan Vyasa, and a revered sage.
Parasurama	the sixth avatar of Vishnu, the son of Jamadagni was born on earth to get rid of the menace of arrogant kshatriya warriors who were abusing their power. He was also the acharya of Bhishma, Drona and Karna.
Parikshit	the son of Abhimanyu and Uttara, he was pronounced at the monarch when the Pandavas decided to retire to the mountains.
Partha	another name of Arjuna.
Parthasarathy	another name of Krishna, which means the charioteer of Partha (Arjuna)
Parvathi	the mother of the universe, also known as Sati. She is the consort of Lord Shiva

Glossary

	and the mother of both Ganesha and Karthikeya.
Pashupathi-astra	Lord Shiva's divine weapon, presented to Arjuna after his encounter with the great god.
Pradyumna	the son of Krishna, he was killed during the final skirmish in Dwaraka before the sea swallowed Krishna's kingdom.
Pratismriti	divine mantra endowed by Vyasa to Yudhisthira, that will be used by Arjuna to reach the Himalayas within a day.
Pritha	another name of Kunti.
Raavana	king of Lanka who abducted Sita and was killed by Rama. He was also known as a great devotee of Lord Shiva.
Rama	the seventh incarnation of Vishnu and husband of Sita, he was king of Ayodhya and vanquisher of Raavana. Rama lived during Treta Yuga.
Radha	wife of Adhiratha, foster mother of Karna who brought him up. Hence Karna is also known as Radheya.
Radheya	another name of Karna, which means child of Radha.
Rajasuya	a ceremonial sacrifice that must be undertaken by a king who wants to be officially an emperor.
Sahadeva	younger son of Madri, the fifth Pandava was also the son of the Ashwini star.

	Known to be a towering scholar even in his youth.
Salva	lover of Amba who was defeated by Bhishma during the swayamwara of the princesses of the Kasi kingdom.
Salya	brother of Madri, king of the Madra kingdom. He was uncle of the Pandavas but was forced to fight on Duryodhana's side at Kurukshetra, as he accidentally accepted the Kuru prince's hospitality before the war. He also served as Karna's charioteer and was the general of the Kaurava army for a day after Karna's death, he was known as a peerless spear warrior. He will be killed by Yudhisthira during the war.
Samba	son of Krishna and Jambavathi, Samba was known to be reckless and unruly, and played a huge part in the Yadu dynasty's annihilation after being cursed by revered rishis for dressing up as a woman to mock them.
Samsaptaka	a succeed-or-die vow taken to achieve one's mission, without a choice to turn back.
Sanjaya	Dhritarastra's advisor and personal assistant, he was also a student of Vyasa and had the gift of 'divya-drishti', which was the ability to witness events that happen at any distance right in front

	of him. This gift allowed Sanjaya to experience the war first hand, and he narrated the same events to the blind king every day.
Saugandhika	a celestial flower that grew in Kubera garden, the very same flower that Bhima procured for Draupadi after meeting Hanuman.
Satyaki	a fearsome Yadu warrior who was one of Krishna's closest friends. He was always outspoken, and was one of the very few survivors of the Kurukshetra war.
Satyavati	wife of Shantanu, mother of Vyasa and great-grandmother of the Pandavas and Kauravas. She was the daughter of a fishermen chief.
Shakuni	prince of the Gandhara kingdom and brother of Gandhari. He was uncle of Duryodhana and largely-accepted as the evil presence in the Kuru prince's mind. He played the game of dice on behalf of the Kuru prince which effectively exiled the Pandavas for 13 years.
Shantanu	famed monarch of Hastinapura, he was father of Bhishma and also the ancestor of the Pandavas and Kauravas.
Shiva	the great god, Mahadeva. He will meet Arjuna and test him before presenting the Pandava with his very-own Pashupathi-astra weapon.

Sikhandin	a woman-turned-man warrior due to penances, who caused the death of Bhishma on the battlefield. Drupada's offspring Sikhandin was Amba in his previous life, and was reborn with a vow to take revenge on Bhishma for the suffering Amba had suffered. He will be killed by Ashwatthama during the night massacre after the war had ended.
Subhadra	sister of Krishna and wife of Arjuna. She was also the mother of Abhimanyu.
Sudarshana	Krishna's spinning chakra weapon, it means wheel of auspicious vision.
Surya	the sun-god, father of Karna.
Susharma	monarch of Trigarta, he will undertake the samsaptaka vow when challenging Arjuna at Kurukshetra. He will be killed by Arjuna.
Swarga	one of the heavenly realms.
Ugrasena	king of Mathura and the Yadavas, and grandfather of Krishna. He will be imprisoned by Kamsa before Krishna killed his evil uncle and released his grandfather.
Ulupi	mother of Iravan and wife of Arjuna, she was the daughter of the Naga king Kauravya.
Uttara (princess)	daughter of King Virata and wife of Abhimanyu, she was the mother of

	Parikshit who would become emperor of the kingdom when the Pandavas decided to leave for the mountains.
Vaayu	the wind-god, he was father of Bhima and Hanuman.
Varanasi	another name of the ancient city of Kasi. Also known as Benares.
Varuna	the god of the oceans, he is also a Lokapala.
Varuna-astra	Varuna's celestial weapon.
Vasistha	a famous sage, his ceremonial cow Nandhini will be stolen by a group of Vasus, leading to him cursing them to be born as mortals on earth. The Vasu that stole the cow was Bhishma.
Vasudeva	father of Krishna, he was also brother of Kunti.
Vichitravirya	the second son of Satyavati and Shantanu, he was the grandfather of the Kauravas and Pandavas. He died childless due to an illness.
Vidura	born from the union of Vyasa and a hand-servant of Ambika, the wise Vidura was considered the most trusted advisor in the king's court, and is a well-wisher of both the Pandavas and Kauravas. He is believed to be an incarnation of Yama who was cursed to take human form for punishing a child's ignorant mistake.

Glossary

Vikarna — son of Dhritarastra and Gandhari, he was Duryodhana's younger brother who advocated dharma. He was one of the those within the Kauravas that objected to Draupadi's harsh treatment by Duryodhana and Duhsasana. He was killed by Bhima during the war.

Virata — king of the Matsya kingdom who unknowingly hosted the Pandavas during their thirteenth year in exile when they lived incognito in his kingdom. He was also father of princess Uttara, wife of Abhimanyu. He will be killed by Drona during the war.

Vrindavan — the city where Krishna grew up as a cowherd with brother Balarama, under the care of father Nanda Maharaja and mother Yasoda.

Vyasa — the celebrated compiler of the Mahabharata, he was son of the sage Parasara and Satyavati, and grandson of sage Vasistha. He would help father Dhritarastra, Pandu and Vidura as both Chitrangada and Vichitravirya would die childless.

Yama — the god of death and justice, also known as Dharma.

Yudhisthira — the first Pandava, also known as Dharmaputra as he was the son of Dharma, the god of justice. Yudhisthira

	is famous for his truthfulness and righteousness.
Yuga	an age or era, it started with Satya Yuga followed by Treta Yuga, Dwapara Yuga and finally the Kali Yuga. It is believed that Vishnu will be reincarnate as Kalki at the end of Kali Yuga.
Yuyutsu	the son of Dhritarastra and his wife Gandhari's maid, Yuyutsu is known as an impartial, moral-adhering character. He will fight on behalf of the Pandavas during the war, and will be one of the few survivors from the war. He will be appointed as the regent of the kingdom to assist Parikshit when the Pandavas chose to retire to the mountains.

ACKNOWLEDGEMENTS

The journey of writing and publishing this book was the combined effort of many, in numerous different ways. Allow me to thank them now.

I would like to thank my family, especially my father, who has always allowed me the freedom to pursue what I felt was right, for which I am always indebted for. And my mother, for the upbringing that I have had from a very young age, it has made me who I am today. Thankful I am for this foundation that I have had – else I might not have even picked up my first version of the Mahabharata, which was ironically my mother's.

My friends, a big thank you for your faith in me and the constant encouragement I received from each and every one of you as I embarked on this journey to write and publish my first book.

I am entirely grateful to my publisher Notion Press, for guiding me throughout the process of publishing this book. I will always be grateful for the support I received, and it was certainly an experience.

Acknowledgements

A special mention for my best friend, Surya, who has been and always will be a huge part of my life. Thank you for always being the joy that you are.

Keeping the best for last as always, thank you Krishna for always blessing me with so much and allowing me to complete this piece of work, which I fully dedicate to You. Our conversations keep me going, every single day.